RULE #11: YOU CAN'T IGNORE YOUR FAMILY FEUD

THE RULES OF LOVE BOOK 11

ANNE-MARIE MEYER

Copyright © 2019 by Amy Meyer

All rights reserved.

No part of this book may be reproduced in any form or by any electronic or mechanical means, including information storage and retrieval systems, without written permission from the author, except for the use of brief quotations in a book review.

To all who believe that Christmas books can be read year round.
You, are my people.

"Bella, I never stopped caring."

LOGAN

CHAPTER ONE

Bella

"Summer is made for relaxing, Bella," my best friend, Gigi, said as she stretched out on the lawn chair she'd dragged into the middle of my backyard. She had on this skimpy yellow bikini that barely covered...anything and sunglasses perched on her nose.

She'd gone all old-school and folded tinfoil over an old cardboard box to use as a reflector.

I snorted as I uncrossed my legs and stretched them out in front of me. It was a hot August afternoon in Sweet Mountain, North Carolina, and I was trying as hard as I could to focus on my homework in front of me.

I only had one week until school started. Which meant one week until my senior year started. If I wanted any chance of qualifying for the scholarship I needed to get into Harvard, I needed a 4.0 GPA.

And I needed to go to Harvard. I needed out of this small town and away from my family, which was falling apart. Dad was gone, and Mom was currently passed out on the couch. I didn't have to ask to know she'd spent the night drinking. Our living room smelled like a distillery.

That may have been one of the reasons we were lounging outside in ninety-degree weather.

I hated being in my house. Always.

"I don't have time for fun," I said as I shot her an exasperated look. With my life, I couldn't even remember what fun was.

Gigi snapped her gum as she shifted in her seat. "You only live once, Bella. Make it good."

I sighed. If only I had her zeal for life. She didn't care about consequences. She was a live-for-now kind of person. We were complete opposites. She was beautiful and graceful. I was a nerdy perfectionist. I cared about grades and extracurriculars, and she cared about makeup and tans.

She fanned herself with the cardboard box and blew out her breath. I didn't think I'd ever understand her desire to develop skin cancer. It made no sense. When I brought it up, she told me I'd never understand beauty. And she was right about that. I was simple. Nothing too spectacular about me. My hair was long. My cheekbones—regular. I lacked anything that made anyone, anything.

Except soccer. I rocked at soccer. And maybe my grades. I was smart, so what else did I need?

I tucked my dark brown hair behind my ear and hunched over the calculus book in front of me. The shade from the tree above helped cool me down as I stared at my notebook. "Harvard students don't have time to have a life." I pulled my hair off my neck and fanned the sweat that had begun to form. I reached over and grabbed my now lukewarm lemonade and took a sip.

Gigi sighed as she set down her sun reflector and swung her ridiculously long legs over the side of the lawn chair. She took off her sunglasses and stared me down. "Let's do something," she declared. She inspected something on her shoulder and moved to flick it away. Then she glanced back at me. "I'm bored."

I furrowed my brow. "I don't have time. Mr. Klaton wants these problems done before school starts," I said, writing the next answer.

"Mr. Klaton is a communist," Gigi said. She leaned her elbows on her thighs and clapped her hands together a few times. I could feel her gaze on me, and after a few seconds, I relented and looked up. Her eyebrows were furrowed as if that would convince me to move.

"What?" I asked.

"It's summer. It's hot. I don't want to sit here and watch you do this." She chewed her lip as she pretended to write furiously on her hand. "I want to go to the pool."

I was unimpressed as I sat back and wrapped my arm

around my knees, hugging my legs to my chest. I rocked a few times before I sighed and nodded. "I'll agree if—"

Her shriek cut through my words, so I paused, waiting for her to finish. Finally, she pinched her lips and nodded at me. "I'm done," she whispered.

I leaned forward and closed my book. Then I stood and wiped off the back of my shorts. "I was saying I'll go if you promise we can leave after two hours." I glanced down at my watch and took note of where that would leave me with time.

I had soccer practice tonight and then dinner by myself while Mom complained about our life, about Dad, and about the Cartwright family—who were the reason the creditors were knocking on our door and all we had was instant ramen in our cupboards.

If I wanted to get this set of problems done today, then…I glanced up to the sky. I could handle taking a break for a few hours.

Gigi didn't seem to notice my hesitation. She had slipped on her swimsuit cover and was tucking her magazine and phone into her purse. "Let's go," she squealed as she slipped her feet into her flip-flops and stood. "I'm so ready to cool off at the pool."

I started to groan—water and I didn't mix—but I stopped when she shot me a look. I knew I was being a crappy friend, so I forced a smile and raised my fists in the air. "Yay, the pool," I said.

If Gigi picked up on my sarcasm, she didn't say

anything. "Let's get you changed into something that's not a t-shirt from the fourth grade and your dad's cutoff jeans."

I glanced down at my baggy clothes—my comfortable baggy clothes—and then back over to her. There was no way I wanted to go back into the house. I didn't know where Mom was or what state she was in.

But that right there was one reason why Gigi and I were still friends. She knew my dirt, and she still stuck around. She wasn't scared of my family or the drama that went with them.

She was the only person I could be myself around.

"I like my clothes," I said as I reached down and picked up my books. After I shoved them into my backpack, I moved to zip it, only to have Gigi pushing at my back.

"Come on, zip and walk," she said.

I sighed but obeyed.

When we stepped into the house, the hair on the back of my neck stood up as I glanced around. My ears perked as I listened for any sign of Mom.

When we passed by the living room and I saw that the couch had been vacated, I blew out my breath. She was either in her room, in the bathroom, or out. Right now, not being around me was where I wanted her.

Once we were inside my room, Gigi spared no time as she marched over to my dresser and pulled out my red two-piece. I parted my lips to protest, but she didn't look the least bit interested.

"You've had this suit for over a year, it's time to try it out."

The sound that emerged from my lips rivaled a sputtering car engine. I wanted to say something. I wanted to object, but I knew it was futile. My mouth had given up before I even had the chance to speak.

I collapsed on my bed and folded my arms. Gigi pointed her fingers from her eyes to me and then to the bikini she'd placed on the bed. Then she turned and left, shutting the door with a resounding thud on her way out.

I sighed as I stood. I knew she wasn't going to let this go.

I bought the bikini last year when I was desperately trying to impress Miller Hardwell. But that had deflated faster than a helium balloon in below-zero weather.

He wasn't interested. And I was left with a broken heart and an itsy-bitsy teeny-weeny bikini.

That was why I didn't try. Why be disappointed over and over again? I had my brain, and I had soccer. There was nothing else I needed.

I changed quickly and then pulled my t-shirt and shorts over my swimsuit. Gigi wanted me to wear the bikini, but she said nothing about covering it up. When I pulled open the door, her eyebrows went up.

I held up my hands and smiled. "It's on. It's on."

Gigi ran her gaze over me and then sighed as she turned and made her way down the stairs. She had her hand in her purse, and I could only assume she was grabbing her keys.

"You're hopeless, Bella Davenport," she said.

I chuckled as I followed after her. "But you love me?" I asked. We'd been friends since kindergarten. We were opposites, but I guess our history made up for personality quirks.

She snorted as we stepped out into the blazing sun. When we got to her convertible, we opened the doors and climbed in.

It took fifteen minutes to get to the Sweet Mountain community pool. There were two winding slides on either side. As a kid, they had been fun. But once you passed one hundred pounds, they become missile-shooting death traps. Especially since one was completely enclosed, which made it impossible to sit up. You spent twenty terrifying seconds getting splashed in the face and feeling as if your body was being torn apart.

And at the end? A major wedgie.

Not my idea of a party.

We climbed out of the car and slammed the doors behind us. With the beach a five-hour drive from our town, we had to resort to the pool. It wasn't the greatest, but it was all we could afford.

Gigi swung her bag over her shoulder as we walked toward the entrance. I kept in step with her as we approached Jordan, a junior at Sweet Mountain High and the goalie on my team. My smile spread as I met her gaze.

"Hey, guys," she said as she reached up and tightened her ponytail. "Wanting to cool off?"

Gigi nodded and snapped her gum. "Nerd over here had her nose in her textbook. It took some convincing, but I dragged her away. I'm melting like a popsicle."

"Nerd? Nose in a book? That doesn't sound like our Bella," Jordan said with a huge smile. She rang us up and then handed us the wristbands.

I shot her an annoyed look, and she just grinned harder. Just as we turned to walk away, she called after us. "Hey, did you guys hear the news?"

I paused and glanced over my shoulder. "What news?" Had something happened to the team? To the school?

A look I couldn't quite interpret passed over her face. It was like if excitement and intrigue had a baby. I raised my eyebrows, wondering what the heck she would be so cryptic about, but then a voice—a very familiar voice—spoke up from behind me.

"Well, if it isn't Bella Davenport," Logan Cartwright's unmistakable voice caused a fire to ignite in my stomach.

I whipped around to meet his—*crap*. He'd grown. A lot. And not just in height. He was...muscular. His dark hair was longer. It fell over his forehead, and he had to shake his head to fling it to the side.

I stared at his familiar blue eyes. They danced with amusement as he stared down at me. His perfectly white teeth shone against his tanned skin as he raised his eyebrows. He was expecting a response from me, but I wasn't going to give him the satisfaction of one.

Not after what his dad did to my dad. Not after what he did to me.

There was one person in my life who could die and I wouldn't care—that person was Logan Cartwright.

My cheeks were on fire as I stared at him. My mind was swirling with every insult I could think of to hurl his way. But none of them came out. It was like my tongue had turned to glue and cemented itself onto the roof of my mouth.

"When did you get back?" Gigi asked. She obviously wasn't struggling as much as I was. In fact, she looked completely at ease as she stared at him.

Logan flicked his gaze in her direction then back to me. He pushed his hand through his hair and shrugged. "My dad made me move back last week. He's taking over Cartwright Fishing International. I'm here 'cause Mom and him will be overseas. I'm staying with my gran."

The entire time he spoke, I could feel his gaze on me, like he was staring me down. And that just angered me more. Who was he to just waltz back into Sweet Mountain like nothing had happened?

We were enemies. Our families hated each other. Sweet Mountain was my turf. When his father cheated my dad out of his cut of the business and stole my dad's invention on top of that, everything had ended in a metaphorical bloodbath.

When they'd packed up and moved, we held a party. An actual party, with invites that read *In Celebration of the Cartwright's Leaving*. I'm not saying it was the best attended party ever—I felt like people were too scared of what might happen if they didn't come. But it made my parents happy—for a moment—even if it also made them feared.

"Looking good, Bella," he said as he took a moment to rake his gaze over me.

I folded my arms in front of my chest and glared at him. He was such a jerk. Such a player. The fact that he was back was sending me on a Tilt-A-Whirl that made my stomach ache.

"Ah, you're still mad." He glanced over at Gigi. "She still hates me."

Gigi nodded as she snapped her gum. "Yeah, well, your family did a jerky thing." She shrugged. "You kind of deserve it."

A flash of something—maybe regret—passed over Logan's face. But as quickly as it came, it disappeared. I let it go. There was no way I was going to stand here and try to interpret how he felt.

I wasn't going to give him headspace like that.

Logan sighed. Someone behind us called his name, and he glanced up and waved. "Well, it's been a blast catching up, but I gotta go." He moved to step around me, and just as he did, I felt a thump on my back. Like he'd patted me or something. Startled, I jolted forward.

When I whipped around, he called over his shoulder, "Don't take life so seriously, Bells."

I parted my lips, anticipating an incredible comeback, but the only thing that I managed to utter was, "You..." and then my brain fell flat.

Furious, I glanced over at Gigi, who looked a little too amused. I glared at her as I wrinkled my nose. "What?" I asked, turning to march toward the turnstiles that led into the pool.

Gigi laughed. "Nothing. You just...I've never seen you come to a complete halt before. I mean, it was like watching a mime. You moved but said nothing."

I glared at her as I flashed my wristband at the person standing guard, and she waved me through. Once we were inside the pool area, we walked over to the lockers. We stripped down to our swimsuits, and for the first time ever, I was kind of glad I'd listened to Gigi.

Wearing this swimsuit with Logan here felt like payback in and of itself. He'd changed a lot since his family packed up and left—but so had I.

And my changes weren't half bad.

We shoved our things into a locker, and Gigi locked the door. I slipped my sunglasses on, and for a moment, allowed my gaze to slip over to where Logan was pulling off his t-shirt.

Sweat began to form on my brow—and I wasn't sure if it was from the heat or the way Logan's muscles rippled when he moved. I grabbed Gigi's hand and pulled her to the pool. I needed the cool water to slap some sense into me.

If Logan was back in Sweet Mountain, that meant one thing: I needed to be on my guard at all times. Getting lost in his grown-into looks wasn't going to help me.

He was the enemy.

CHAPTER TWO

Logan

I kept my gaze on Trenton as he droned on and on about soccer and how the team was pumped that I was back. I nodded and smiled, but all my body wanted to do was peek over at Bella.

Things had changed since the last time I saw her. Things had changed *a lot*. No longer was she some lanky girl with glasses and frizzy hair. Now she was... Heat rose inside of me, and I pushed those thoughts from my mind. There was no way I could think of Bella like that.

Our families hated each other. And there was some feud between our parents. But if you asked me, it was all ridiculous.

What had happened, happened. It was in the past, and it didn't involve either of us. So the fact that Bella seemed determined to defend her parents' honor was annoying, if kind of cute.

She was passionate. She always had been. And I was a little bit excited that she hadn't changed in that department.

"Dude, are you listening to me?" Trenton asked.

I glanced over at him and shrugged, my signature *I-don't-care-about-the-world* smile spreading across my lips. "Of course, man. But you're kind of droning on and on. Let's just go swimming. We can connect and sing Kumbaya later."

I took off to the pool's edge, and once I hit the deep end, I dove into the icy cold water. With the temperature outside in the high nineties, it felt amazing.

Once I rose to the surface, I flipped to my back and floated, staring up at the sky.

I'd never planned on coming back to Sweet Mountain. My parents had promised a cushy life in New York. Cartwright Fishing was doing well. Why not climb the social ladder?

Things had started to change six months ago. Mom wasn't sleeping, and Dad was drinking a little too much. When they finally called me into Dad's office and told me things were bad, it only confirmed what I'd already suspected.

Their trip to Paris to find an investor was the last straw. If it didn't work, we could kiss everything we'd grown accustomed to goodbye.

RULE #11: YOU CAN'T IGNORE YOUR FAMILY FEUD

So here I was, back in the hometown my parents had screwed over. Thankfully, Gran wasn't high maintenance. She loved her cribbage group and couponing at the local grocery store. She let me do what I wanted, which was nice.

I flicked my feet to get myself moving, and, in the process, bumped into someone. They grunted, and I shifted in the water to see who it was. But before I could turn, she spoke.

"Hey, watch it." Bella's voice broke through my thoughts.

I smiled as I lowered my feet and stood. I turned and was faced with Bella's angry gaze once more. Her hair was wet and clung to her skin. Her dark eyes narrowed as she glared at me.

I bent closer to her and met her gaze. Her eyes widened as she took a step back. "It's a crowded pool, Davenport. It's bound to happen."

Her lips parted, and I couldn't help but notice how perfectly formed they were. Her little cupid's bow looked so kissable, and the daggers she was throwing my direction? Well, they only endeared her to me that much more.

It was a challenge, and I wouldn't be a true Cartwright if I didn't love a challenge.

She seemed to be at a loss for words, so I shrugged, winked, and pushed back into the water. I heard her say something to Gigi, but I didn't take the time to try to listen. Instead, I closed my eyes and felt my body relax.

Senior year was going to be interesting. I wondered how the rest of the student body would respond to my return. I understood Bella's reaction, with all of our history. But did they all hate me?

I knew I wanted things to return to normal. I wanted my old life back. My New York prep school was cliché and boring. I hated being there. Hated wearing the uniform. Plus, their soccer team stunk. And besides acting like I didn't care about anything, playing soccer was the only joy in my life.

Feeling ridiculous for getting all emotional about my future, I made my way over to the ladder and climbed out. I was ready to shoot down one of the slides at peel-your-face-off speed.

That would help me get my mind off school, my parents, and most of all, Bella.

THANKFULLY, I managed to avoid the ice queen all afternoon. After I'd slid down the slide a million times, Trenton said he was ready for some food, so we both climbed out of the pool and headed to the concession stand.

I stood in line, dripping wet, enjoying the feeling of the breeze on my skin. It was a nice contrast to the blistering sun. Trenton was talking—again. This time, it was

RULE #11: YOU CAN'T IGNORE YOUR FAMILY FEUD   17

about how he couldn't wait to see the team's faces when we walked into practice tomorrow.

"They're going to crap their pants," he said with a laugh.

Apparently, Spencer had taken over as team captain when I left, and, according to Trenton, he sucked. Last season they didn't win one game. But this year was going to be the Panther's comeback. With me on the team, we were sure to rack up victories.

"Nice," I said as I nodded. I wasn't sure what to say. I'd left, and the team had had to make up for my loss. But if I were truly honest, I was enjoying the fact that the team seemed to miss me. That I was an asset somewhere, even if it wasn't with my own family.

Before I allowed myself to get lost in my ridiculous reverie, a very loud voice sliced through my thoughts. I blinked and turned to see Tanya Pickering standing a few feet off.

"Logan?" she asked, er, yelled, "Logan Cartwright?"

I glanced around to see that every mom and her toddler was staring at me. Their eyes were wide as if they weren't sure how to take Tanya's outburst.

I pushed my hands through my hair, spraying water everywhere, and then stepped out of line. I knew coming face-to-face with my ex-girlfriend was inevitable. I just didn't think it would be this fast. "Hey, Tanya," I said.

She blinked a few times before she squealed and leapt into my arms. I stumbled as I tried to catch her, and her lips slammed against mine. Her hands clawed at my hair, and I just stood there, shocked.

When she pulled back, she giggled. Finally able to breathe again, I set her down and stepped a good foot away from her. There was no way I wanted to experience that again.

"How's it going?" I asked.

She smiled and twirled her hair with her finger. She hadn't changed. She was still the same girl that I had broken up with when I left. Everything about her was perfect—except her personality. She was annoying and dull. I'd moved on.

"Shocked," she said as she sidled over and wrapped her arm around my waist. "I can't believe you didn't call me." She smacked my chest and giggled, again.

We made our way back in line, where Trenton was holding my spot. Tanya seemed stuck to me like glue. No matter what I did, she wouldn't let go. So I stood there, my relaxing afternoon quickly changing into a blast from the past.

"I just got back," I said as I shot a *help me* look in Trenton's direction.

He just chuckled as he moved forward with the line. Realizing that my friend wasn't going to do anything, I took in a deep breath and told myself to chill. After all, she couldn't stay glued to me forever, right? At some point, she was going to need to let me go. I could hold out until she grew bored.

RULE #11: YOU CAN'T IGNORE YOUR FAMILY FEUD   19

We moved with the line, and all the while Tanya chatted on and on about how she was relieved that I was here. She was disappointed with the lack of decent guys in Sweet Mountain. And her plan to be homecoming queen was in the bag now that I was back.

I nodded but didn't really respond. Instead, my gaze found its way over to Bella, who was sitting at a far table with Gigi, a stack of nachos in front of her. She was laughing at something Gigi had said, and I couldn't help but stare.

She was beautiful. More than I'd remembered. We'd been friends once. Back when our parents were in business together. Things had been easy between us. Until my dad screwed her family over.

As much as I didn't want to admit it. As much as it made me feel weak and vulnerable to even think it—I'd missed her.

Maybe leaving Sweet Mountain had changed me. Made me realize what was important. We'd chosen the cushy life, and it came back to bite us. Nothing felt as good as being friends with Bella. And I hadn't noticed until just now, watching her laugh as freely as she'd once done with me.

"Hello? Earth to Logan." Tanya said as she snapped her fingers in front of my face.

I blinked a few times but kept my gaze trained on Bella. A few moments later, she glanced up and met my gaze. I offered her an apologetic smile, but her lips dropped into a frown, and she focused her attention back on her nachos.

I sighed and looked over to Tanya, who looked very annoyed that I was ignoring her.

"What?" I asked. We stepped up to the cashier, who had just finished handing change to the woman in front of me.

"I was talking to you about homecoming, but you weren't listening." She jutted out her lip and pouted at me.

I sighed, ordered two hotdogs and a Coke, and paid. I stepped off to the side to wait for my food while Tanya ordered a Diet Coke and an apple.

I rested my elbow on the counter, and as soon as my food was dropped off, I grabbed it, told Trenton I was headed to a table, and hurried away from Tanya—before she glommed back onto me.

I picked a table that was a few spots away from Bella and slipped onto a seat. Just as I was about to take a big bite of my hotdog, Tanya appeared. She sighed as she collapsed on the seat next to me.

"I'm thinking we need to start doing some recon work," she said. The fizz from her Diet Coke hissed as she twisted the lid.

I busied myself—and my mouth—with eating. I knew she was waiting for a response, so I just nodded along with her as she went on and on about getting matching clothes, where we would go for dinner, and how we were going to clinch the titles of homecoming king and queen.

I wanted to tell her she was ridiculous. I couldn't understand why she was so obsessed with being homecoming queen. It didn't amount to anything in the real world. After all, once high school was over, we were all moving on with our lives.

It didn't make sense to put so much time and effort into something that didn't matter in the long run. But I knew if I voiced my real opinion, whining would ensue, and right now that was the last thing I wanted. So I kept quiet and nodded along with whatever she said.

Thankfully, she didn't seem to notice when my gaze slipped over to Bella, who seemed to be done with her nachos. She had her feet up on the seat next to her and was resting her chin on her knees. I could see her smile as she chatted with Gigi, and for a moment, I wondered what it would be like to be the recipient of her smile— instead of the frown she always seemed to have for me.

The hardest part of our situation—the status quo our parents left us with—was that I remembered what it was like to be friends with Bella. To be a part of her half-baked schemes.

She used to be so fun. So relaxed. Until the feud of the century. Now, she was tighter. Drawn in on herself.

I could feel it in the air around her. I could see it in the slump of her back. It was like she had the weight of the world on her shoulders, and she wasn't willing to let go.

The thought made me incredibly sad. Happy Bella was fun. Happy Bella was carefree. Holding onto her parents' anger was dumb. What happened had nothing to do with her. It had nothing to do with me.

I chuckled as I shook my head. Maybe coming back to Sweet Mountain was exactly what I'd needed to do. Perhaps it was my job to bring her back. To help her shed her anger and move on.

I was going to melt that icy heart of Bella Davenport, or I was going to die trying.

CHAPTER THREE

Bella

I got home from the pool and showered the chlorine off of me. Just as I was pulling on my sweatpants and t-shirt, I heard the front door open, and an icy feeling settled in around me.

I swallowed as tears pricked my eyes. Someone was home. Mom or Dad, it didn't really matter. Whoever it was, they'd changed. Our family had changed.

After pulling my hair into a bun on the top of my head, I swallowed and somehow found the strength to rest my hand on the door handle and turn it.

I was making progress.

Normally, when there were other life forms in the house, I hid out in my room. Where I was safe. Where I didn't incur the wrath of Mom or Dad. But I was hungry and dying of thirst. Swallowing my spit wasn't cutting it anymore.

Just before I slipped out into the hallway, words carried from the kitchen, freezing my feet.

"Sam, where have you been?" Mom's voice was high-pitched and desperate. There was a slur to her words that told me she wasn't sober.

"Leave me alone," Dad said. His voice was low and gruff. It no longer had the ease that it used to back when things were simpler.

"Were you with her?" Mom's voice rose an octave, and I heard some scuffling. I didn't have to see what was happening to play the scene out in my mind.

Dad would be hunched over the counter, making food. Mom would be standing near him, begging him to give her an answer. Begging him to stay.

Then Dad would have enough of her interrogation, grab his wallet and keys, make his way to the back door, and disappear for days. Mom would desperately claw at his arm, waist, leg—anything to keep him from walking out the door. Again.

She would drown herself in alcohol. And I would be here. Always here. In my room, trying to figure out how to live my new life.

Alone.

Right on cue, the back door slammed, followed by a sob. I closed my door and rested my back against it, tipping my face toward the ceiling and slamming my eyes shut.

RULE #11: YOU CAN'T IGNORE YOUR FAMILY FEUD

I wasn't going to cry about this. I'd already done enough of that. With my eyes closed, those traitorous tears couldn't fall. They were the only symbol of the pain raging inside of me.

The pain no one knew about.

I wasn't sure how long Mom stayed in the kitchen. I finally made my way over to my bed and collapsed on top of it. When I woke up at midnight with a scratchy throat and the need to pee, I finally tiptoed out of my room.

Mom was nowhere to be seen. It didn't surprise me that neither of my parents took it upon themselves to see if I was home. Or even alive.

I grabbed a banana and a water bottle and slipped back to my room. After I ate, I crawled under my blankets and curled up with every pillow in my room.

As I lay there, staring up at the lights reflecting from the street, I felt a single tear slip down my face. I blinked and cursed myself for being so weak.

Crying didn't change anything. Crying didn't bring my family back. All crying did was wet my pillow and make me feel weak. And I wasn't weak.

The moment I let my wall down, I knew I was going to break. For my survival it had to stay up. If even a small part began to crumble, I was done. I wouldn't be able to come back from that.

I couldn't have that happen. I was going to leave this place one way or the other. I had to.

THE WALLS in Coach Meyer's office felt as if they were closing in on me as I stood in front of her desk the next day. I knew she was saying something as I watched her lips move, but the ringing in my ears drowned out her words.

All it took was her saying "Work with" and "Logan Cartwright" to cause my body to spasm and my entire world spin like I was on the Tilt-A-Whirl at the annual Sweet Mountain carnival. I should have never answered her phone call. I should have never come in to see her.

I blinked a few times and heard Coach Meyer clear her throat. Her eyebrows were raised, and her lips were pinched together. She was waiting for me to respond.

I swallowed—my mouth had turned insanely dry—and took in a deep breath. "I'm sorry, will you repeat that?" I mumbled. I hated it when my teachers were disappointed in me, and ignoring Coach was not the way to get on her all-star list.

She cleared her throat and handed a piece of paper to me. "Listen, Bella. I'm completely aware of what happened between your families. I know it's going to be hard for you. But..."

She paused and looked conflicted. Then she nodded her head resolutely and turned her attention back to me. "Honestly put, I don't care. This is a once-in-a-lifetime chance, and we need all hands on deck. All the money you and Logan can raise will help offset the cost of plane tickets for the entire team. Getting everyone to Brazil is above your families' petty issues."

Her words felt like daggers through my chest. I knew a lot of people in town were tired of hearing about how the Cartwrights screwed over the Davenports. But that didn't mean that our lives hadn't been destroyed.

The town may be ready to move on, but we weren't. I wasn't. It wasn't even a blip on our radar.

I numbly took the paper from her and stared down at the writing. With how clouded my brain was, it looked like Egyptian hieroglyphs instead of the English language. I folded it methodically and shoved it into my back pocket. I'd read it later.

"So, do you think this is something you can go along with?" Coach asked as she leaned against her desk and folded her arms. She stretched her legs out in front of her and stared me down.

I swallowed, my tongue sticking to the roof of my mouth. Somehow, my body must have completely forgotten how to produce spit.

"I'll try," I whispered and forced a nod that I was pretty sure looked jerky and out of control.

Coach looked at me for a moment and then reached down to grab her hat and whistle. "That's all I can ask for," she said as she rested her clipboard on her hip. "Come on, the girls are waiting."

I nodded as I followed after her. The reverberations of my steps rattled through my body as we made our way out of her office, down the hall, and through the large metal doors that opened up to the practice field.

I opened and closed my lips so many times, I was sure I looked like an oxygen-starved fish. I wanted to come up with an airtight reason as to why it was a bad idea for Logan and me to work together. I wanted her to agree with me. To say I wasn't crazy to hate Logan as much as I did.

But Coach's irritated expression and pinched lips told me she wasn't interested. My feelings were ridiculous, and I should just get over it. If she only knew how much I wished I could. How much I wished that my family life wasn't in the crapper.

Maybe the town had moved on, but my life was stuck on repeat. It was Groundhog Day over and over again. For me, there was no *getting over it*. I wasn't even sure what that would look like.

My family was in ashes. My whole life felt like a whirlpool in a crap storm. I was spinning and spinning and going nowhere.

We got to the bench, and I set down my stuff and ran out to the field where my teammates were stretching.

Mandatory summer practices always made me smile. For everyone else, it was time away from the pool or the Falls—a place where kids went to hang out. For me, it was a break from my house. A break from studying. And a break from my life.

I lived for the field.

The more I practiced, the less energy I had to obsess about my home life and getting into Harvard.

I was going to be the success that they felt they lost. I had to prove to them that a Davenport could pick herself up and make something of herself.

Which was why, despite how I felt about Coach Meyer's news, I was going to figure out a way to work with Logan. After all, being team captain was important for my college application. And if I put up too much of a stink about Logan, I was pretty sure Coach wouldn't have a problem switching me out for Tessa Woodworth—who had never been shy about her desire for my spot.

Plus, the fact that Coach seemed convinced I wasn't going to do this drove my competitive spirit. And the thought that Logan had assumed I wouldn't do it either lit a fire inside of me.

I was going to prove them wrong.

I was not only going to raise all the money for our tickets, I was going to do it alongside Logan.

AFTER PRACTICE, I showered and dressed. I was pulling my hair up into a ponytail as I pushed open the locker room door and ran straight into Logan.

I yelped and stumbled, but my hands were too tangled up in my hair to free themselves in time. I braced for impact.

Instead, I felt two very warm and very large hands surround my waist, and suddenly, I was pressed against Logan's chest.

His solid chest.

My entire body heated from embarrassment as I used every available appendage to push away from him. My elbows. My knees. I wiggled and moved, but no amount of pushing freed me from his grasp.

I was sure that my hair was a ratted mess, and my face was glistening with sweat as I finally settled down and glared at him.

"You can let me go," I growled. Why was my heart pounding? And why was he still touching me?

This was not okay. At all.

Logan chuckled as he met my gaze. "Do you think that's wise?" He nodded toward my tangled hands.

I glowered at him and tried not to wince as I pulled my fingers free. Then I raised my hands. "See? All good."

He raised his eyebrows, and his ridiculous smile remained on his lips as he stepped back. "Geez, remind me not to save you from sudden death," he said as he hoisted his duffle bag farther up his shoulder and turned away from me.

Frustrated that he was, one, walking away from me and, two, blaming me for the fall that he'd caused by startling me. And maybe him thinking he'd had the last word irked me too. "Excuse me," I said as I hurried after him. I tried to rake the gnarls out of my hair so I didn't sound *and look* crazy.

Logan didn't pause. He quickened his pace as if he were trying to outrun me.

Ha. I'd seen him on the field, and I was pretty sure I was faster.

"Excuse me," I said again as I sprinted and turned so that I was standing in front of him—effectively blocking his retreat.

He paused, glanced down at me, and then sighed. "What do you want, Davenport?"

I parted my lips, but the flash of anger—or regret—that raced through his gaze made me stop. He didn't look like the cocky boy who had strutted out of here last year. He looked...broken.

Which was stupid. What could have broken him? His parents won the lottery when they took my father's invention and made hundreds of millions.

I pushed out any sympathy that had risen up inside of me and scowled. His expression didn't change as he continued to study me.

"I, um..." My brain halted. Maybe I needed to see a doctor. This was happening a lot. "Did Coach Larson talk to you?" I finally asked.

He sighed, and his stance softened as he leaned back and scrubbed his face. "Yep."

Heat permeated my cheeks. I was hoping for more of a reaction. Was he mad? Did he hate this as much as I did?

"And?" I stared up at him.

He met my gaze and shrugged. "What do you want me to say? I hate the idea?"

I knew he was mocking me, and it was irritating, but I wasn't going to let up. "It's a little ridiculous, right?"

Why was it when I mentioned our families' situation, people looked at me like I had two heads? They looked at me like my feelings about what happened were no longer justified.

How had everyone, especially Logan, moved on already?

"Bells, come on. It's just a fundraiser. The teams will be there. Are you telling me you can't move past this" —he waved his hand between us— "in order to help the teams go to Brazil?"

I glowered at him, hating that he was right. Working together didn't mean we had to see each other. Or speak. And there would be other people there as a buffer.

My body relaxed as I felt the adrenaline whoosh from my body. I liked what he said—but I hated that it came from him.

I peeked up at him and nodded. "Okay, I can do that."

He studied me and then smiled. This one I didn't quite recognize. It was soft and...understanding? I blinked a few times. First my ability to speak, and now my eyesight was going. I definitely needed to get my head checked.

"Good. I'm happy we've come to an agreement," he

RULE #11: YOU CAN'T IGNORE YOUR FAMILY FEUD

said. "Now, I've gotta go help my grandma move some furniture around. Do you mind?"

"Yeah, sure. Sorry," I said as I stepped out of his way.

He ducked his head and moved past but then paused and turned to look at me. His brows were furrowed as he searched my face—or my soul. Whichever it was, it sent a shiver up my back. "I want you to know, I didn't come back to fight." His voice was low, and I believed what he was saying.

I parted my lips and said the first thing that came to my mind. "I don't want to fight either." Just as the words left my lips, I paused.

My brain was trying to convince my heart that what I'd said was a lie. But there was a part of me—a very teeny tiny part of me—that knew it was the truth. Logan wasn't his father. My current situation *wasn't* because of Logan.

You can't help where you come from. I would hate it if people judged me by my parents. I was so much more than what they'd become.

I shoved those thoughts aside and focused my attention on Logan. He studied me for a moment before he sighed and turned away. "You need to work on your acting skills, Davenport," he said as he shouldered his bag and took off down the hall.

I stood there, staring at his back. I watched as he pushed through the outside door and disappeared around the corner. I scoffed and turned my attention to the ceiling. I blinked a few times, hating that my eyes burned. Hating that I felt bad for hating Logan as much as I did.

His family hurt me. *His* family hurt *my* family. That wasn't something I could just move on from. My entire life had changed. Nothing was the same. I was a ship lost in a massive storm, and I had no idea where I was supposed to go.

The fact that he felt he could blow back into town and everything was going to be fine—that everything was forgiven—was ridiculous of him.

"*You're* bad at acting," I murmured as I straightened and finished pulling my hair up into a bun.

Even though he wasn't there to hear my lackluster comeback, saying the words did make me feel better.

If he was going to call me out on my lie, I was going to call him out on his. No matter how much he said he didn't come back to fight, I knew the truth. Logan Cartwright wasn't over our family feud. Not a chance.

I wasn't going to be the only crazy, grudge-holding person at school. Logan was just as bad as I was. I was just going to have to figure out how to pull it out of him.

CHAPTER FOUR

Logan

Gran was sitting in her recliner when I finally made my way into her house later that evening. Trenton had insisted on heading out to the Falls, so I stupidly went along. I should have known it was a bonehead move.

There was nothing there but girls and booze—not my scene. I'd had enough of that in New York to last me a lifetime. Nothing good ever came from that combination—especially when I was involved.

I stuck to the edge of the group, hoping to keep a low profile. But Tanya found me and remained glued to my side the entire time. Which I guess was a good thing. None of the other girls dared the wrath of Tanya.

Lucky for me, I was able to pull Trenton away from his friends two hours later, and I dropped him off at his house and headed home. I'd have to take him back to the Falls tomorrow to pick up his car. There was no way I was letting him drive home drunk.

But, being around him, seeing the kind of person he'd become, left a sour taste in my mouth. Sure, we were pretty much adults—even though we weren't legal—but that didn't matter. When Trenton drank, he became a major jerk, and I saw a side of him that hadn't been there a year ago.

It made me sad, the idea that things had changed. I guess it was foolish to think that life would stay still in your hometown. That no matter how long you were gone, you could always come back to the way it was. That felt like a pipe dream now. The proof was right in front of me.

Everything had changed.

I shut the front door and made my way across the living room. Gran glanced over at me as she tipped her wine glass to her lips and took a sip. She eyed me, her gaze sweeping over me as she assessed the state I was in.

I sighed as I collapsed on the couch and stretched my legs out. "Don't worry, no alcohol."

She muttered a mm-hmm as she set her glass down. "Don't lie to me, boy."

I scrubbed my face then tipped my head back to rest on the back of the couch. My body began to relax as I took in a few deep breaths. "Z, Y, X, W, V..." I tipped my head forward and gave her sly smile.

Gran chuckled and pushed her recliner closed. "Smart aleck," she said as she slowly stood.

I moved to stand, only to have her wave me away.

"I ain't old, child," she said as she rested her hand on her back and pressed her body to standing.

I snorted and settled back in my seat. "Sure."

She shot a dagger-like look my direction and then shuffled over to the kitchen. I heard some banging of pots and pans. I knew what she was doing, and I hated that she was doing it. I didn't want to inconvenience her. She'd already done so much for me, and I felt like a jerk grandson already.

I stood and made my way into the kitchen to find her standing in front of the stove. There was a pot of water heating up and an open box of pasta next to her.

"Gran, I can make my own dinner," I said as I moved closer to her. Just as I reached for the box of pasta, a wooden spoon came down on my knuckles.

"What do you think you're doing?" she asked.

I rubbed my hand and faked a hurt expression. "Getting beat by my grandmother," I said as I gave her a sarcastic look.

She chuckled. "It's the one thing I can do. Let this old woman cook dinner for you."

I studied her, trying to force away the guilty feelings. "Fine." I pulled myself up onto the counter and watched as she salted the water.

For some reason—for the fiftieth time that day—my

thoughts returned to Bella. I couldn't get her out of my mind. She was adorable when she glared at me. And I had to admit I was excited that we were paired to help fundraise for the trip to Brazil.

All I wanted to do going into my senior year was move forward from this ridiculous feud between our families. I was so over everything, and if working together helped us move on, I was all for it.

Gran got out a container of grapes and opened them next to me to start rinsing them in the sink. I snagged a couple while narrowly missing her swat.

"Logan," she said.

I shrugged as I popped one into my mouth.

She shot me a disgusted look. "They weren't washed."

"Eh, I like to live a little." As I chewed, I thought about how I was going to ask my next question. I didn't want to raise any flags, and I certainly didn't want her getting the wrong idea.

I decided to stop overanalyzing things and just take a shot.

"Funny story, Bella Davenport and I were assigned to work together on a fundraiser for the soccer team," I said slowly, keeping my gaze down. I didn't want Gran to think I was eager. Or that I might have conflicting feelings about any of this.

Gran slowed and stood there with her gaze turned down. Then she moved to stir the pasta in the pot. "Davenport?" she asked.

RULE #11: YOU CAN'T IGNORE YOUR FAMILY FEUD

I nodded. I knew she didn't need to be reminded of what had happened. It was pretty engrained in everyone's mind.

Her lips were pinched as she turned to face me. "It's better for you to stay away from her."

I sighed and gave her a look that I hoped told her I was over this nonsense. She met my gaze head-on. She may be a tiny woman with bright white hair, but she was formidable when she wanted to be.

"Really? Come on, I'm sure they've gotten over it." I popped the last grape I'd stolen into my mouth and then glanced around for more. She'd set the rinsed grapes on a plate, and I leaned across the counter and scooted them closer.

"Gotten over it?" Gran snorted as she stuck the ladle into the pot and pulled out a noodle. She munched on it thoughtfully and adjusted the heat on the stove.

"What your father did..." Her voice drifted off as a sense of sadness washed over the room. She dropped her gaze and wrung her hands. "The Davenports haven't been the same since. Sam is a no-show, and Jocelyn? She's a ghost of a woman when I see her."

Gran began to open and close the cupboards and didn't stop until she pulled out the strainer. She stuck it in the sink and padded over to the stove.

Gran's words rolled around in my mind as I thought about what she said. I knew things were bad in the Davenport household, I just didn't know they were that bad.

I watched the steam billow up in front of Gran as she drained the spaghetti and mixed in some sauce. We didn't talk about Bella or the Davenports the rest of the evening. I could tell Gran didn't want to discuss it further, and I wasn't about to push.

All I knew was, no matter what, I wanted to put what was in the past behind us.

I would make it my mission to mend things between the Davenports and the Cartwrights if it was the last thing I did before I graduated.

After all, what did I have to lose?

I STOOD outside the school the next morning in sunglasses and swim trunks. Coach Larson had specified the terms of the fundraiser. We were to rally our teams together and host a car wash at the abandoned parking lot located on the corner of Main and Unity. All the money we could muster up would go to putting a dent in the cost of the plane tickets.

We were to work as a team, no matter what.

I tapped my fingers on my crossed arms as I stared down the road, waiting for Bella to join me. The team captains were supposed to meet a few hours before the other members showed up to make sure we had all the supplies. Lucky for me, Coach Larson seemed just as

RULE #11: YOU CAN'T IGNORE YOUR FAMILY FEUD

eager to have me back as Trenton, and after I scored the tenth goal, he declared me the new captain.

Glancing down at my phone, I sighed. Bella was already a half hour late.

I snapped my gum and pushed off my car. Frustrated and bored, I reached down and picked up a rock. I rolled it around in my fingers a few times before I chucked it into the bushes.

After I threw all the available rocks, I scrubbed my face and got into my car. I was done waiting. If Bella wasn't going to show up, that was her choice. If she wanted to sink the girls' team, I wasn't going to stand in her way.

But I wouldn't be some chump waiting for her anymore. I was going to do what I could to send the boys' team to Brazil. Coach Larson said to be a team player, but how could I do that when I was paired with someone determined to bring me down? I was sure he'd understand.

I shoved my keys into the ignition and pulled out of the parking lot. Frustration brewed inside of me. Was Bella intentionally screwing me over?

I guess I'd always figured that she was smart. That she knew where to draw the line. But maybe I was wrong. Maybe she did hate my family so much that she was willing to sabotage me.

I'd come back thinking things could change, but maybe they couldn't.

I flipped on my blinker and turned down Main Street.

I was a few seconds away from the lot we'd rented to host the car wash. I pulled in and parked toward the back. I contemplated parking my car in front so it looked like we had business, but then decided against it. I was lazy and knew eventually I'd have to move it.

Coach Larson had dropped off all the supplies last night, and I'd packed them in my car. Poster board, paint, and brushes to make signs. Soap and rags to wash the cars.

After I pulled my keys from the ignition, I tucked them under the front seat and popped the trunk. I tucked as much stuff under my arms as I could and began to unload.

I dumped the items off to the side, and once the trunk was empty, I slammed the hood and dusted off my hands. Sweat dripped down my back, and I lifted up the collar of my shirt and wiped my face.

It was already nearing ninety degrees at eleven o'clock, which meant today was going to be a scorcher. I was grateful that we were going to spend the day getting wet.

Just as I began to lay out the poster board, I heard the crunch of gravel behind me. I glanced over my shoulder and my heart rate picked up speed—from frustration only.

Bella was finally here.

I stood and squinted, raising my hand to cover my eyes so I could get a better view of her—and to make sure she saw the frustration on my face.

When I finally caught a glimpse of her in the driver's seat, my resolve to hate her waned. She was staring straight ahead with her brow furrowed. Her lips were pulled tight, and she looked...sad.

I swallowed as I watched her pull past me and park just behind my car. I busied myself getting the paint ready to make the signs, but I angled myself so I could see what she was doing. A few seconds passed before she opened her door and stepped out.

Her legs looked long in the shorts she was wearing with a flowy floral top and red flip-flops. Her hair was piled on top of her head, and just as she stepped out, she slipped on a pair of sunglasses.

She glanced around, and for a moment, I felt her gaze land on me. But then she busied herself with removing things from the back seat of her car. With her arms full, she swished her hip and slammed the door shut.

I turned to face her as she approached, and I realized that what she was carrying had begun to slip. Her knuckles were white as she gripped onto the bottles of soap that were slowly sliding down the sides of her body.

I contemplated waiting to see how she got out of this situation, but then I felt like a jerk. Even if she was convinced that I was a prick who would stand back and watch a girl struggle, I wasn't going to solidify that conviction.

I strode over to her and grabbed one of the soap jugs before it hit the ground. Even though I could feel Bella's resistance, I didn't care. She was going to take my help whether she wanted to or not.

"I can do this," she mumbled.

I shrugged as I removed a few more things from her arms and brought them over to where I'd stashed the supplies from Coach Larson. I could hear her huff and follow after me.

It gave me a nice sense of satisfaction.

After all, she was the one who was late. I'd waited half an hour for her. If carrying some of her things annoyed her, I had half a mind to carry *her* across the parking lot.

"I had them," she said.

I paused and then stood. She sounded close. Not really thinking, I turned to face her. I'd been right. She was only a few inches away from me. My sudden movement must have startled her. She blinked a few times, and her lips parted like she was gearing up to scold me, but nothing came out.

She just stared at me.

For a moment, I allowed myself to get lost in her dark brown eyes. "It's okay to take help sometimes," I said as I held her gaze. Then slowly, ever so slowly, I leaned in.

When she didn't say anything, I paused and allowed my cocky smile to emerge. Things were feeling a little too intense; I needed to bring us back to earth. Then I winked, turned away from her and focused back on the signs I was painting.

I heard her scoff and murmur something under her breath, but I didn't acknowledge it. I had the upper hand with her right now, and I wasn't about to let that go. Who knew what would happen between us in a few minutes? I knew Bella wasn't done with me, but for now, I was going to bask in my win.

Bella's wall was going to come down, even if it was one brick at a time.

CHAPTER FIVE

Bella

Logan Cartwright.

Logan *freaking* Cartwright.

There were no words for how I felt about him. Anger. Annoyance. Another feeling I wasn't quite ready to acknowledge, although it did feel a lot like nerves. Apparently, my body felt like it was a good idea to let a million butterflies loose in my stomach every time he was around.

It must be my worry that he was going to suddenly take everything I owned and skip town with it—like father like son—that had my entire nervous system on edge.

It couldn't be anything else.

I blew out my breath as I turned to focus on the stuff for the car wash laid out in front of me. We had an hour of prep time left before the other members of the team

RULE #11: YOU CAN'T IGNORE YOUR FAMILY FEUD   47

started showing up. I wanted to be ready so we could get the next few hours done. Then I could get the heck away from Logan and his cocky smile, which he was currently casting my direction.

I narrowed my eyes at him and shook my head as I turned away.

What was with him? He was smiling and *winking* at me. It felt playful, but it also felt a little condescending. Who did he think he was? And what was his angle?

I was late this morning because Mom had a meltdown. Like, wine in hand, sobbing on the kitchen floor meltdown. Dad hadn't come back last night. When Mom checked his credit card activity, it said he was at a hotel in Virginia.

He'd driven hours to sleep somewhere else. Away from his family. Away from his life.

I tried to help Mom, but moving a hundred-and-fifty-pound woman by yourself is no easy task. I ended up sitting on the floor next to her, handing her tissues while she cried. Then she fell asleep, and all I could do was get her a pillow and blanket and leave her right where I found her. After placing a cup of water and two painkillers for her to find when she woke up, I left.

I stopped for a chocolate shake—I was in desperate need of anything chocolate—and pulled into the parking lot to find Logan glaring at me.

Of course.

The world revolved around Logan. What would he

know of heartbreak? Of watching your family fall apart right before you and feeling powerless to stop it?

That was how I felt right now. Powerless.

I glared down at the sign I was working on as I felt tears prick my eyes. I blinked, hoping to push them back in. There was no way I was breaking down in front of Logan. Thankfully, I had sunglasses on, which hid my momentary lapse of control.

If I could just get a grip on my life, I might survive my senior year.

From the corner of my eye, I saw Logan glance over at me a few times. It was like he sensed something was wrong. His cocky smile had morphed into a stoic expression. He was concerned about me, and I wasn't sure how I felt about that.

"Everything okay?" he asked and reached over to paint the *h* on *carwash*.

I cleared my throat and nodded. "Yeah. Of course. Why wouldn't it be?" Then I pinched my lips. Why did I respond three different ways? People who were fine just gave one response.

He didn't answer right away. He finished painting bubbles on his sign and then scooted over to work on another one. Feeling like a loser who didn't know how to communicate, I swallowed and focused on painting a car on my sign. "You?"

I saw him pause and glance over at me. "Me?" he asked, like he was genuinely surprised.

I nodded. "Yeah. It's customary to ask how the other person is doing." My cheeks felt like they were going to burst into flames. I had half a mind to strip down to my swimsuit and douse myself with water.

Why was having a conversation with Logan this hard?

"I just figured you didn't care," he said.

"I don't," I blurted and then pinched my lips together. "Sorry."

Logan was full-on staring at me now. He had sat back with his forearms resting on his knees. I wasn't sure what to do under his scrutiny, so I continued painting the same spot over and over again.

"Doesn't it get tiring?"

His question caught me off guard, and I ended up streaking paint across the board. I sighed. Talking and painting wasn't going to work. If I didn't want to ruin every sign, I needed to focus.

So I sat back and turned my attention to him. "What?"

He'd pulled off his sunglasses and held my gaze for a moment before he scrubbed his face. "Holding the torch for your family." His voice was low, and I had to lean in to make sure I heard him.

"Holding what torch?" Heat began to prick at the back of my neck as realization dawned on me.

He scoffed and reached down to pick up some gravel and roll it around in his hand. Then he glanced toward the road and chucked the gravel at the sidewalk. "This ridiculous feud between our families. Isn't it time to…move on?"

The world around me began to fade as I stared at Logan. Then a flash of Mom passed out on the kitchen floor surrounded by used tissues entered my mind. Get over it? Was he serious? How could I get over something that completely and utterly changed my life?

What was I supposed to go back to? A normal life?

Newsflash, Logan, I didn't have a normal life to go back to. It was only a matter of time before Mom and Dad called it quits. Then what would I have?

Hopefully, they would wait until after I graduated. After I got accepted into Harvard. Then, I could leave and never look back. And they could decide how they were going to continue on with their crappy lives.

But no, there was no moving on for me.

Not anymore.

Frustrated, I focused my attention back on the sign. I'd been the idiot who attempted to speak to him. I should have just left things the way they were.

Call me crazy, but my current situation was not something I wanted Logan to be privy to. He'd ruined *my* life.

He didn't deserve to learn anything about me.

He must have picked up on my mood, because he didn't push it further. Instead, he became studious and focused back on his sign. I felt my shoulders relax, and my body began to calm.

We moved together as we busied ourselves with getting ready. I could stand next to him or hand him something without any issues. But when it came to talking, I was out.

I wasn't interested in hearing what he had to say, and I definitely didn't want him hearing what I had to say. If he just stood there, I was fine.

Or at least, I *would* be fine.

I glanced down at my watch and saw that we had about ten minutes before the other team members were going to show up. I reached up and tightened my bun as I glanced around. Things were coming together.

Logan had hooked up the hose to the building next to the lot. I'd laid out the buckets and measured out the soap. Then Logan went after me and filled each one with water. The sponges and rags were laid out, and the signs were dry and stacked against the building.

We were ready.

I stood there, fiddling with the hem of my shirt when I felt Logan approach me. My entire body tightened as he neared. I waited for him to say something. To do something. But he just stood there.

Taking in a deep breath, I tipped my head to the side to peek at him. His arms were folded across his chest, and he was staring straight ahead. His jaw muscles flexed as if he were fighting with what he wanted to say.

I sighed and focused on the street as well. I wasn't sure I wanted to know what he was thinking. Every time he opened his mouth, I became more confused and frustrated.

"I'm sorry," he said.

Every part of my body froze as my brain registered his words. My tongue felt heavy in my mouth as I swallowed. Did he just say what I thought he said?

Before I could respond, a thumping bass turned up way too loud filled the air, and Trenton Massey's car came into view. Logan whooped and jogged over to greet his friend, leaving me to stand there, stunned.

I swallowed as I wrapped my arms around my chest and focused on taking some deep breaths. This was crazy. *I* was crazy. Why did I agree to do this carwash? Maybe Harvard wasn't that big of a deal. Maybe I could survive another year here if it meant I didn't have to work with Logan again.

But giving up on my dreams—of Logan taking yet another dream away from me—made me quesy. I pushed that idea way, *way* down.

No. I wasn't going to let Logan, or anyone else, derail me. I was going to succeed. I had to.

I called Gigi and asked her to come down to the lot. As soon as I mentioned shirtless guys washing her car, she jumped right on it, proclaiming she'd see me in ten minutes.

By the time she pulled into the lot, the car wash was in full swing. I'd been right. I didn't have to talk to Logan at all once the car wash opened.

We decided on a little friendly competition and split up, boys against girls. My team was ready to wipe the floors with the boys. We were competitive. You didn't get to be state champs by sitting down.

Gigi honked her horn, and I waved at her as she pulled in behind Kate, who was listening to music as we scrubbed her car down with soap. I'd given up on my top and was wearing my swimsuit with shorts.

Half the boys' soccer team had stripped down to their trunks, garnering mostly female business. I rolled my eyes as I allowed my gaze to wander over to Logan to see that he still had his shirt on.

Of course, he had to be different. Even when I heard a few girls shout at him to take it off, he just winked at them and smiled. Then he flexed his arms, and I rolled my eyes.

Out of nowhere, he glanced over at me. His gaze softened, and he winked.

I dropped my gaze back to Kate's car. I wiped the final bits of dirt off, and then Kari, one of our team's midfielders, sprayed the car with the hose. Once she was done, we all grabbed rags and began drying the car.

Sweat ran down my face, and I wiped it from my eyes with my wrist. I was determined to get this car washed and start the next one up before the boys finished. Just as I wiped away the final streak, I heard cheering coming from the guys' side.

When I glanced over, my heart rate picked up speed. Logan was up on the hood of the car they were cleaning, dancing and slowly pulling off his shirt. All the girls around me stopped and turned to stare.

I blinked as I watched him expose his stomach—are eight-packs a thing?—and then his chest, and finally pull his shirt over his head. He swung his shirt above him a few times while all the girls who had congregated around the car screamed. Then he threw the shirt, and before I could move, it smacked me in the face.

The cold, wet shirt of Logan Cartwright *smacked* me in the face.

I stepped back a few feet as I tried to get my bearings. Through the chanting and cheering, I heard a curse and the sound of Logan jumping to the ground.

Embarrassment. Anger. Frustration. They all coursed threw me as I pulled the shirt from my head and turned to run. Once I was behind the building, I leaned my back against the warm brick and covered my face.

Hitting me with his wet, gross t-shirt was a new low, even for him. I didn't want them to, but tears began to slip down my cheeks as I tipped my face toward the sky.

I was so completely lost that I didn't know what was happening. First, Logan says he's sorry. Then he flirts with anything with two legs and breasts. And now? He throws his shirt at me and embarrasses me in front of the entire town.

If completely and utterly humiliating me was what he wanted, he won. The gold medal goes to Logan Cartwright.

I was broken, and I hadn't thought I could break any more.

Apparently, I was wrong.

"I'm so sorry." Logan's voice cut through my thoughts.

I stifled my sob as I glanced over at him, angrily wiping my tears from my cheeks. His gaze roamed my face, and for a moment, it looked as if he felt guilty. But I pushed that idea away before I let it confuse me more.

"Why are you here?" I asked as I wrapped my arms around my chest and glared at him. I feared that if I let go, my broken heart would fall and bleed out on the cement.

Logan parted his lips as he stared at me. Then he slowly started to shake his head. "It was a mistake. An accident. I would have never—"

"Stop. Please," I said and closed my eyes. A traitorous tear rolled down my cheek as I sucked in my breath. "Why did you have to come back? Why couldn't you have just stayed away?"

When Logan didn't respond, I feared that he'd left, and I looked like an idiot standing there talking to a wall. When I opened my eyes, I found him staring at the ground with his brow furrowed. He was pushing his hand through his wet hair, making it stand on end.

He must have felt my gaze on him, because a moment later he glanced up. "Is that what you want? Me to leave?"

A sob slipped out, and I nodded, squeezing my arms tighter around my chest. Why did everything hurt? Why wasn't any of this making me feel better? He broke me. He broke my family.

But I had no right to tell him where he could or

couldn't live. I cleared my throat. "Just stay away from me, please," I managed.

Logan studied me then sighed as he nodded. "I promise." He turned and started to walk toward the carwash. As he passed me, he stopped but didn't look up. He kept his gaze trained on the ground.

"I'm sorry, Bella. I hope you know that."

My entire body felt as if it were breaking. I couldn't physically respond. All I could do was nod.

As much as I wanted to believe that what he said was a lie, I wasn't so sure anymore. Logan was a flirt and, apparently, had horrible aim. But I was beginning to believe something that I'd never thought possible.

Logan was sorry.

Truly sorry.

What was I supposed to do with that information? Even though I didn't want to, a part of me—and it was growing bigger every minute—believed that what he said was true. Which left a shaky, conflicted feeling inside of me.

If he was sorry, then everything I'd brought myself to believe about him was wrong. Was that something I was willing to face? I wasn't so sure anymore.

I'd lived with my anger for so long that the threat of having it taken away scared me. More than anything else in the world.

If I didn't hate Logan, who was I?

Was I really ready to face that person?

CHAPTER SIX

Logan

I was a jerk. A bumbling jerk.

Why did I think it was a good idea to strip off my shirt and throw it?

Sure, the girls had been were cheering for it. And sure, it did feel a little satisfying when Bella looked as well. But only I could take a broken person and make them feel lower.

The look on her face as she pulled the shirt down would forever be burned in my mind. I'd hurt Bella. And that wasn't sitting well with me.

Every time I saw her, a rush of emotions coursed through my body. Emotions that I was pretty sure went above and beyond *just frenemies*.

I sighed as I reached out and dried the Chevy Malibu

in front of me. The sun was setting behind the trees, and our car wash was winding down. I peeked over at the girls to see that they were finishing their last car as well.

I stepped away from the car we were working on as Trenton gathered the payment from the driver, then the car pulled away. We busied ourselves with cleaning up, and as the girls' last car drove away, they did the same.

The rest of the girls' team didn't seem to feel the same about us as Bella felt about me. They worked together, laughing and flirting as they all cleaned up. A few tried to talk to me, but I just smiled and moved on. I wasn't interested, and the last thing I wanted was to string them along.

Wanting a break from all the chatter, I grabbed some buckets and walked over to the line of trees behind the building next to us. I let out a sigh as I dropped the buckets and straightened.

It felt good to stand there. The sun was disappearing, which meant the temperature was dropping. A breeze even picked up and cooled my skin. I stretched my arms over my head and leaned from one side to the other.

I glanced to the side and spotted Bella. She was sitting on the ground a few feet away, staring off into the trees. She had a stack of empty buckets next to her. Apparently, we'd had the same thought.

I swallowed. The desire to talk to her rose up inside of me, but I realized that would be a mistake. Bella had made it pretty clear that she wanted nothing to do with me. I might as well get that through my head.

RULE #11: YOU CAN'T IGNORE YOUR FAMILY FEUD 59

A shrill sound filled the air, and I glanced over to see Bella pick up her phone. She studied it and furrowed her brow. Then she pressed talk and brought her phone to her ear.

"Hello?" she asked.

I knelt down and began tipping the buckets over so the water ran into the grass. I felt her gaze, and, from the corner of my eye, I saw her shift so that her back was to me.

"Yes, she is," she muttered.

I kept my gaze forward as I continued emptying the buckets. I didn't want to eavesdrop, but I also wanted to stay and find out what was going on. And it wasn't just to learn what Bella was so desperately keeping from me.

Something was wrong. I knew Bella, and I knew when she was worried or attempting to face something by herself. Her confident demeanor was slipping. I could see it in her shoulders and hear it in the tone of her voice.

"Okay. I'll be there in ten minutes to get her," she whispered.

I busied myself with stacking the buckets as Bella hung up and moved to stand. She glanced over at me for a moment before she let out a dramatic sigh, picked up the buckets, and walked back to where the other girls were finishing up cleaning.

I picked up my buckets and returned to where the guys had just finished. They were going to the local diner for dinner and invited me. I glanced over at Bella, who had just refused the girls' invitation, and politely declined.

Something was up, and sitting around with my teammates, listening to them laugh and joke, wasn't going to erase the image of Bella's deflated demeanor. I'd finish helping her clean up and then head home to spend some time with Gran. And maybe, I'd find the confidence to approach Bella again.

Five minutes later, Bella and I were alone. I stuffed the wad of cash Trenton had given me into my pocket and leaned down to gather the rest of the supplies. I glanced over in Bella's direction, only to see her glancing in mine. I slowed, hoping it wasn't too obvious that I was waiting for her to catch up.

I couldn't help but wonder if there was something more going on than simply Bella's hatred for me. And there was this stupid part of me that couldn't seem to let that thought go. And an even stupider part of me that thought I could actually help.

When she passed by me, I hurried to fall into step with her. I swallowed, my throat suddenly turning dry as I contemplated what I was going to say.

I forced my fear from my mind and spoke up. "Have a hot date?"

Bella stopped walking as her entire body tightened.

Warning bells went off in my mind, and I regretted trying to approach her so soon after she basically told me that she wished I'd never been born. Man, I was glutton for punishment, that was for sure.

Bella glanced over at me and sighed. "What?" she asked as she made her way over to her trunk.

I wished a hole would open up and swallow me entirely. But I followed behind her as I conjured up my best *I-don't-care-what-you-think* response.

"You didn't go out with the girls, and earlier, on the phone..." I said as I raised my eyebrows and motioned toward the trees.

Bella dumped the supplies into her trunk then turned with her hands on her hips. "Do you make it a habit of listening to other's conversations?" Her eyes narrowed as her gaze met mine head-on.

I scoffed and shook my head. "I just overheard. No eavesdropping here."

Bella reached up and gripped her trunk then slammed it closed. Then she walked past me and over to the driver's door. "I'm late," she said as she pulled open her door and climbed in.

I wanted to ask her what she was late for. I wanted to learn more about Bella, but she wasn't having it; instead, she slammed her door and started her engine. A second later, she pulled out of the parking lot and onto Main Street, leaving me staring after her.

I groaned as her taillights faded from view. Well, that went over about as well as a fart in church. Bella was consistent, I'd give her that. She was not going to budge about any of this. She was determined to hate me for all time, and I couldn't see that changing anytime soon.

I finished cleaning up and climbed into my car. I pulled out of the parking lot and headed down the road. With the radio on, I rolled the window down, allowing the night air to rush in.

I took a few deep breaths and relaxed in my seat. My wrist rested on top of the steering wheel as my mind wandered from Bella, to her family, to what she was doing right now.

I'd never given someone this much space in my brain before, but I didn't really feel like I had a choice. She was crowding out everything else in my mind. For some reason, all I could think about was her.

I rounded the bend on the outskirts of town when a parked car caught my eye. I blinked a few times in the settling darkness as I realized it was Bella's car. She was crouched down by one of her back wheels.

Instinct took over, and I pulled in behind her. She straightened and squinted at me as she raised her hand to cover her eyes. I left my engine running and my lights on as I unbuckled and pulled open the door.

I must have been hard to see with the lights behind me, because I'd never had Bella stare at me so hard for so long. When I was a few feet in front of her, she groaned and turned away. Not letting that deter me, I walked over and crouched down so I could see what was wrong.

"I have it under control," she said, her voice breaking.

RULE #11: YOU CAN'T IGNORE YOUR FAMILY FEUD

I nodded. She'd pulled out a car jack, and I bent over as I tried to locate the best place to put it.

"Logan," she said. I could hear the desperation in her voice.

I glanced up at her before I continued with the jack. She was so stubborn that she wasn't going to allow me to help change her tire? Seriously?

Well, I could be stubborn as well. When it came to who wore it best, I was going to win.

Once I had the jack in the right spot, I sat up and started looking for a tire iron so that I could loosen the lug nuts.

"Here," she said, holding the tire iron in front of my face. "Since you insist on staying."

I glanced over at her as I took it. Bella's face had fallen and her gaze was downturned. As soon as she was no longer holding the tire iron, she folded her arms across her chest and her shoulders slumped.

I nodded and began to loosen the lug nuts. Everything was going according to plan until I got to the fifth nut. No matter what I did—no matter how hard I tried, I couldn't get it loose.

Noise from the back seat drew my attention, and suddenly, Bella was in my face. She looked desperate as she glanced at the tire. "Are you almost done?" she asked.

I flicked my gaze over to the backseat window and then back to her. "I don't think I can get this last nut loose," I said as I attempted to loosen it again.

She dropped down next to me and leaned in. Her arm brushed against mine, causing goosebumps to ripple across my skin. Warmth rushed up my arm and exploded in my stomach.

"You can't get it loose?" she asked. She turned to look at me, her eyes wide.

Not wanting to discover what my voice sounded like after a touch from Bella, I just nodded.

"No, no, no," she whispered as she moved to stand.

Why was she so upset? I straightened and turned my attention to her. "It's fine. I'll just call Tony and he can give you a tow."

"What's the point of all those muscles if you can't loosen a lug nut?" Her words caught me off guard, and—with her pinched lips and flushed cheeks—they had caught her off guard as well.

I decided to just roll with it. "Well, I'm strong, but I'm not the Hulk," I said with a wink.

She looked shocked for a moment, but that wore off quick, and she was back to glaring at me. "Why do you keep doing that?" she asked. I must have rattled her because she started pacing next to me.

I tried to loosen the lug nut again. "Do what, Bella?"

"Wink at me."

I paused. I hadn't expected that. "Wink at you?" I asked as I sat back so I could focus on her.

She nodded. "Yes."

"Does it bother you?" I asked as I began to tighten the

lug nuts I'd loosened. No matter what she thought of my strength, there was no way I was going to be able to move the last one, and I didn't want her to lose any of the others.

When she didn't answer, I glanced over at her. She'd stopped. Her face was pale, and she was staring at the rear window of her car. From the corner of my eye, I saw something move in her back seat.

Was someone in there?

I stood and peered down at her. "Are you okay?" I asked.

She pinched her lips and blinked a few times. Then she glanced up at me. Tears had formed on her eyelids. "Can you just get it loosened?" Her voice was so low, so broken, that it caused a protective reaction to rise up inside of me.

I'd never had this strong of a desire to fix a tire in my entire life. But I was only human. I could only do so much.

"How about I just give you a ride?" I asked as I stepped closer to her.

Her eyes widened, and she instantly stepped back. "No, you can't," she whispered.

I shot her an annoyed look. "Really? It's just a ride into town. I don't think it will kill you." I moved closer to her again. Eventually she was going to have to stop moving away from me. I'd wear her down. I was pretty sure of it.

A tear slid down her cheek as she shook her head. "Yes, it will."

That felt like a punch to the gut. I dropped my gaze for a moment; then I focused back on her.

"Why would that kill you?" I hadn't intended my voice to come out so low and intense. And for some reason, I was okay with it. Especially since it seemed to catch Bella off guard.

"Because..." For a moment, she held my gaze.

In that moment, I saw everything she didn't want people to see. I saw the kink in her armor. I saw her fear. Her pain.

A surge of desire to wrap her in my arms and take all of that away jolted through me. I found myself unable to move. I didn't want her to push me away. I feared if I stepped back, she'd take that as an opportunity to hoist her wall even higher.

And I didn't want that.

The sound of a car door clicking open broke through the silence, followed by a low groan. Fear flickered in her eyes as she held my gaze then glanced toward the back seat.

I followed her gaze to find her mom's pale face and hollow eyes.

"Bella?" Mrs. Davenport asked before she pitched forward and vomited all over the ground.

CHAPTER SEVEN

Bella

"Mom," I said as I rushed to her. Part of me wanted to make sure she was okay. The other part wanted to shove her into the car, slam the door, and pretend that Logan hadn't seen her.

My secret was out, and fear coursed through my body. What was Logan going to do with this information? Besides Bernie at the pub—and Gigi—no one else knew that things had gotten this bad. I wasn't ready for the circle of trust to include my enemy.

Mom waved my hand away as I approached. She'd finished throwing up and was wiping at her lips. "I'm fine," she said, slurring her words. She pushed off the seat, but her hands were too close to the edge and they slipped off.

Frustrated that she was acting this stubborn when she was drunk off her rocker, I held onto her shoulders and pushed her back into the car and shut the door. I rested my hand on the outside of the car and took in a few deep breaths as I braced myself for what Logan was going to say.

Would he laugh? Mock me? Or worse, would he feel sorry for me? I wasn't sure what he was going to say, but no matter what, the last thing I wanted was for him to realize just how broken I was.

How broken he'd made me.

I coughed as I brought my gaze up to him and shrugged. "I've got it from here. I'll call the tow truck, and he'll pick us up." I forced a grin and waved to his car. "You can go."

His gaze slipped to his car and then back to me as if he needed to clarify what I was saying. Then he glanced over at Mom. I could see her head resting on the back of the seat.

When he didn't say anything, I wanted to scream. What was he thinking? Why couldn't I read his expression? Staying in this limbo was driving me insane.

He walked toward me with a determined look in his eye. I watched as he approached. He didn't stop until he was inches away from me. Of course my traitorous heart began to pound as he neared. I swallowed, my ability to talk—to think—rushed from me. What was I supposed to do? How was I supposed to handle this?

RULE #11: YOU CAN'T IGNORE YOUR FAMILY FEUD   69

"Logan?" I managed through my clouded brain.

He glanced down at me for a moment, and then he was leaning toward to me. His warmth washed over me in a way I'd never felt before. I found myself leaning in too. Wanting to feel more. There was a calm that settled inside of me that caught me by surprise.

"This is ridiculous," he said, his voice was gruff as he stared down at me, then the sound of the door releasing filled the air.

Before I could speak. Before I could ask him what he was doing, he swung the door open and disappeared inside the car. I heard him murmuring to my mom. I blinked, trying to ground myself in the present. A moment later, he reappeared holding my mom's hand as he helped her out.

Her drunkenness had turned to sadness, and tears were streaming down her face. Logan was whispering that everything was okay as he helped her walk to his car. Halfway there, she tripped, but Logan didn't miss a beat. He swept her up and carried her the rest of the way.

He didn't struggle with the door handle of his car, nor did he have an issue with gently setting her on the back seat and buckling her in. After he set her hands on her lap, he shut the door gently next to her.

I was too stunned to speak. I felt frozen in place. All I could do was stare at Logan as he rested both hands on the outside of his car and tipped his head forward. His shoulders sagged, and I couldn't figure out why.

This was my mother. *I* should be embarrassed.

And I was. My entire body was shaking as the realization of what had happened crashed over me. Before I could stop myself, tears began to flow, and I couldn't stop them. There was no more hiding. There was no more pretending that what the Cartwrights did hadn't crushed our family.

He knew everything. Well, he didn't know about Dad, but one look at Mom, and it would be easy to connect the dots.

It was like fate had a pitiless sense of humor. A moment later, the heavens opened and rain began to pour down on me. Not only was I a broken mess, but I was going to look like one too.

I wrapped my arms around my chest as I felt my body fold in on itself. If my legs weren't so stiff, I would have collapsed there on the gravel road. All I needed was a good, strong breeze, and I was going down.

Rain ran down into my eyes as I watched Logan round his car, heading for the trunk. I furrowed my brow as I watched him. What was he doing? He'd already declared my car DOA, I doubted anything he had in his trunk was going to fix that.

When he finally shut the trunk, he had something small and black in his hand. Confused, I watched him walk toward me. His expression was hard to read in the pelting rain.

But I could tell he was staring at me with an intensity that caused my stomach to flip upside down and sideways.

RULE #11: YOU CAN'T IGNORE YOUR FAMILY FEUD

As he reached me, he stuck his hand out to the side, and an umbrella popped open.

Before I could protest, he lifted the umbrella up over my head. He simply stood there, not speaking. All I could feel was his presence. But he didn't say anything. He just stood there and...waited.

I shook as I tried to figure out what to do—what to say. My mind was swirling with questions. I wanted to ask him why he was being so nice. Why he was still here. Why he hadn't left.

I'd been horrible to him. Sure, he deserved a lot of it, but he should hate me.

But it seemed as if he didn't. Instead, he was holding an umbrella over my head and had my drunk mom in the back of his car.

It wasn't fair. I hated him. He needed to hate me back. That's how this worked. If he could just do that, then I could be happy. Or at least, I could pretend that I was happy. I'd forgotten what happiness felt like. I wasn't even sure I could feel that emotion again, but I could pretend.

I was good at pretending. But that required him to do what I expected. It required him to be the person I knew he was. But kind? Helpful? I wasn't sure how to react to that. Not when it came from Logan.

"Whenever you're ready," he finally whispered so quietly that I had to lean in to hear him.

I shifted my eyes up to look at him. His expression was soft as he held my gaze for a moment. Slowly, a half smile emerged. It wasn't his cocky, normal smile. This one was different.

It was almost like he cared.

My knees weakened, and suddenly I began to collapse. Not wanting him to think I needed him to ride up on his white horse, I used the moment to pitch myself forward and stumble toward his car. Great. Now he was going to think that I was no different than my mother. That drunken staggering ran in our family.

Thankfully, he didn't attempt to help me walk. He simply stayed close as he held the umbrella for me while I made my way to the passenger side. I reached out to grab the door handle, but my fingers brushed his as he beat me to it. His touch paralyzed me, and all I could do was watch as his fingers curled around the handle and pulled the door open.

He situated himself so that he could hold the umbrella fully over the door and then glanced down at me. I was pretty sure I looked insanse, standing there just staring at him.

But how could I not? I had not expected any of this. He'd stopped when I was on the side of the road. He'd helped even when I told him I didn't need it. He'd...stayed.

Through this entire horrible day, he didn't leave.

Right now, he had more brownie points than Dad.

Exhausted from trying to figure out his angle, I collapsed on the seat. My tears had subsided, and I used my hands to wipe away the remaining ones, which had mixed with rainwater, from my cheeks.

I couldn't help myself as I watched him round the hood of the car and climb into the driver's side. After he closed his umbrella and slammed the door, he started the engine. He twisted his body to look over his shoulder, his fingers grazed my shoulders as he rested his hand on my seat and pulled away from my car.

Out of instinct, I pulled away, my gaze dropping to his hand.

He pulled away too, noticing my reaction. "Sorry," he mumbled as he pushed the car into drive and took off down the road.

"It's okay," I said. Well, that was a good sign. I at least remembered how to speak. All was not completely lost.

He didn't try to speak to me or ask me questions as we drove to my house. It actually surprised me that he remembered where I lived. He pulled into our driveway and idled the engine as he unbuckled.

"I can handle it from here," I said quickly. There was no way I wanted Logan to give me a ride home *and* come into my house on the same day. There was only so much change I could handle.

His brow was furrowed as he ran his gaze over me. "I do have all the muscles," he said as he pulled the release on the door and stepped out before I could respond.

I sat there, helpless, as he opened the back door, spoke softly to Mom, and helped her out of the car. She murmured something, but it wasn't coherent. Logan hoisted her back up, carried her to the front door, and disappeared inside.

The realization that Logan Cartwright was in my house washed over me, and I became desperate to get him out before he saw too much. I doubted Mom had changed the state of the house for the better, and when I'd left, it looked like a tornado had whipped through.

I hurried to unbuckle and open my door. I sprinted across the lawn and into the house, shutting the door and kicking off my flip-flops.

Logan and Mom weren't in the living room or kitchen. Just as I walked by the stairs, a towel was tossed on me. I stopped as I reached up and grabbed it off my face.

Glancing up, I saw Logan peering down at me with a grin. "I figured this time I'd toss something you actually wanted."

I stared down at the towel, and by the time I looked up, Logan was gone. I wiped my face and toweled my hair as I tried to process what was happening.

Maybe I was dreaming. If that was the case, this was weird dream.

It wasn't like I had never dreamed about Logan before. Maybe in the darkest parts of my mind I'd actually admit that there were moments—fleeting moments—when I allowed myself to think of him romantically. And those fleeting moments showed up in my dreams. When I wasn't conscious enough to push those feelings way, *way* down.

But nothing about this day felt like a dream. Everything felt very real.

I began to grow nervous when Logan didn't come back down. Not wanting him to stay longer than he had to, I climbed the stairs to find him. After checking on Mom, who was lying in bed with a blanket pulled over her, I searched the other rooms. I found Logan standing in my bedroom.

Embarrassment and anger rushed through me as I hurried to usher him out. I didn't want him in my house, much less my bedroom. It was like every wall I'd built up around me, he was trying to tear down.

My room was my last defense. And he was standing there, in the middle of it, glancing around.

"What are you doing?" I asked as I rushed in. His gaze had been trained on my desk. On a picture of Gigi and me last summer at the pool. Back when I was happy. When my life wasn't a complete mess.

Logan blinked a few times as if I'd just snapped him from a trance. He swallowed, and I hated that I noticed the ripple of his jaw muscles as he studied me.

Then, right when I thought he was going to speak to me—right when I was pretty sure that he was going to tear through the wafer-thin wall I had remaining around my heart—he nodded, turned, and walked from the room.

I saw him jogging down the stairs and heard the front door opening and shutting.

And then I was alone. With my disintegrating protection and my drunk mother passed out in the room next to mine. Suddenly, I had no more strength, and all I could do was collapse on my bed and curl up on my side.

Tears flowed as I buried my face into my pillow.

I wasn't sure how long I lay there, crying. But eventually, my body relaxed and the tears stopped coming. Exhaustion took over my body and I closed my eyes and fell asleep.

CHAPTER EIGHT

Logan

The sound of the kitchen sink being turned on pulled me from sleep. I yawned as I stretched out on my bed. With practically no effort, my thoughts went to Bella and what I'd seen last night.

Her mom. Her house. Her wide eyes as she stared up at me like she was afraid I would reach out and crush her. I hadn't realized how much she had been hiding behind that mask she'd put on. Or that things could have gotten this bad.

I was a fool for thinking that she should just get over her issues. How could she? With what she was living with every day, I could only imagine how hard things were for her. How much her life had changed because of my parents' selfish decision.

I growled as I threw off my covers and padded over to the bathroom. After a quick shower, I dressed and found Gran standing in the middle of the kitchen in her robe, frying up bacon. The smell filled my nose, and my mouth began to water.

"Morning," I said as I leaned down to kiss her cheek. I grabbed my keys from the counter and headed toward the back door.

"Where are you going?" she asked in her commanding voice.

I glanced over my shoulder and winked as I reached out and rested my hand on the door handle. "I'm getting someone. Set another place?"

Gran's lips parted and she looked confused, but I didn't stay long enough to hear her response. I jogged over to my car and climbed inside.

I was a man on a mission, and nothing was going to stop me. Bella was convinced that she didn't need anyone in her life, and I was going to prove her wrong.

I doubted I could stop myself. There was something about her that was pulling me in, and I couldn't get her out of my head. And maybe I didn't want to.

Her house was quiet as I pulled up in front. The drapes were pulled closed, but her car was still in the driveway with the spare. I threw my keys up into the air as I walked across her yard and up to the door.

I knocked three times and waited.

Nothing.

Glancing around the door, I peeked through the side window. I saw nothing. No movement, which made me doubt she was even up.

I reached out and pressed the doorbell this time.

Nothing.

Standing there on her stoop, ringing the doorbell to a completely lifeless house started to make me feel ridiculous. What was I doing? Why was I here?

I shoved my hands into my front pockets and bounded down the steps. My car felt so far away, and the heat from my embarrassment pricked at my skin. It didn't help that it was already heating up for the day.

But before I left the steps, I heard the door open. I shoved down all my self-doubt and turned around to find the door open and a very startled Bella staring down at me. Her hair was tousled, and she was wearing a pair of Bugs Bunny pajamas that looked like they had fit her about three years ago.

Despite my best efforts, my gaze dropped to her legs and slowly made its way up to meet hers.

Warmth was rushing through my body, but this time, neither the weather nor my embarrassment was the culprit.

I forced myself to calm down as I climbed back up the stairs and smiled at her. Her eyebrows went up further as she stared at me. Her pouty lips parted, but nothing came out.

"Get dressed," I said as I leaned forward to hold the door I feared she was going to slam in my face.

She jumped back when my chest brushed her arm. I chuckled as her hand immediately went to where we had touched. Her movement made an opening in her doorway, and I took my chance and stepped inside.

"What—wha—?" she stammered as I shut the door behind me.

Now there was no way she could force me out. She was going to have to face me.

"Get dressed," I said again as I smiled at her.

She blinked a few times, and seemed to get her bearings as she folded her arms across her chest and stared me down. "What are you doing here?" she asked.

I leaned my back against the wall. I stretched out my legs then looked up to meet her gaze. "I'm taking you for some breakfast."

She swallowed as she stared at me. I could see her trying to process what I was doing here, what my angle was. I was trying my best to look relaxed and not like a creeper, which was what I feared she thought at this moment.

She squinted. Then she shifted her weight as her hands moved to her hips. I could see the fight flash in her gaze. She wasn't going to make this easy. Which was okay. I had all day.

I didn't want to force her to do something she didn't want to. So I decided on a different tactic. We were friends once. I was pretty sure it was possible for her to like me again.

I straightened and smiled down at her. This one was more genuine. "Come on, it won't kill you to come eat a meal with me. Gran is making bacon. She'll be crushed if you don't come."

Bella's eyebrows went up at the mention of Gran. She was someone Bella adored, and I knew slipping that in would help seal the deal. Bella shifted again, her hand going to her hair as she glanced around. Then her gaze stopped on me and she narrowed her eyes.

"One meal?" she asked as she raised her finger and pointed it at me.

"One meal," I said with a shrug.

She nodded a few times before she blew out her breath. "Okay. Give me five minutes to get dressed."

Before I could say anything, she hurried up the stairs. I couldn't help but watch after her for a moment, before I dropped my gaze and forced my thoughts to return to how the tile below my feet looked.

It felt much longer than five minutes. For a moment, I feared she'd escaped out the window and ran away. Which I wouldn't put past her.

Right when I was going to call the police to report her missing, the sound of her feet on the stairs drew my attention. She looked unsure as she descended, but I couldn't see anything but how amazing she looked in a plain white t-shirt and cutoff shorts.

Her hair was pulled up into a bun, and I could tell that it was damp—she must have showered.

When she reached the bottom, she folded her arms and glanced up at me. I could see the fire in her gaze as she stared me down. "I decided to take my time, seeing as how you barged in here making demands."

I chuckled. I couldn't help it. She was adorable when she was angry. "That's fine. I appreciate it when people smell good." I reached out and grabbed the door handle, which brought me closer to her. I noticed the sweet smell of what must be her shampoo as I did.

"Don't sniff me," she said as she waved me away.

I pulled open the door. "Too late, I already did."

She growled as she grabbed her purse from the side table and shoved the strap up onto her shoulder. "Well, don't do it again," she said as she stormed out of the house.

I followed after her, shutting the door behind me. I half-expected her to wait for me—which was dumb. I could tell from her walk as she stomped across the yard that she wasn't happy with me or the situation.

Lucky for me though, she knew I was determined. If I wanted something, there was a good chance I was going to get it. If she made me, I would camp out on her lawn until she gave in.

I jogged after her so I could beat her to the passenger door. She glared at me, but I just smiled as I reached down and pulled on the door handle.

"After you." I winked and motioned toward the seat.

RULE #11: YOU CAN'T IGNORE YOUR FAMILY FEUD

That just caused Bella to deepen her scowl. "Don't wink at me," she mumbled under her breath as she climbed into the car.

Once she was situated, I shut the door and hurried around the hood. After I got buckled in, I started the engine. But before I backed out of her driveway, I glanced over at her. "So, no sniffing your hair and no winking. Anything else I should stop doing?"

Bella was staring straight ahead, but as my words settled in around us, she glanced over at me and held me gaze. Then she sighed. "What's your angle, Logan?"

Her question caught me off guard. I rested my hands on the steering wheel and studied the dash. Then I put the car in reverse and pulled out. Once we were on the road, I cleared my throat.

"Do I have to have an angle?" I asked. It was frustrating that Bella seemed to think I would only talk to her if I wanted something. Like I was sent back here to torture her. What a frustrating way to live.

"Cartwrights always have an angle," she whispered.

I peeked over at her. Her arms were folded across her chest, and she was staring out the window. Her words were daggers in my heart. This wasn't what I wanted. Not at all.

"Not all Cartwrights have an angle. Some just want to be friends." I kept my gaze forward and focused on the road, but from the corner of my eye, I saw Bella glance over at me.

"Why?" she finally whispered after what felt like an eternity.

I slowed the car to a stop as the light in front of me flashed red. I sighed as I drummed my fingers on the steering wheel and mulled over what I was going to say to her. I wanted to be truthful, but I also didn't want to scare her off.

"I guess I'm tired of torturing myself because of what our parents did—what my parents did." I glanced over and offered her a consolatory smile. "I'm not my parents. I'm far from them." I held her gaze.

Tears welled up in her eyes. I could see how broken she was. For this moment, Bella was allowing me in. My heart began to pound as I realized she was letting her walls down.

But as quickly as the moment came, it went. Bella sniffled and wiped away a tear that had slipped down her cheek. Then she glanced out the window.

We drove in silence the rest of the way to Gran's house. As I pulled into the driveway and turned the car off, Bella seemed to get a handle on her emotions, and she was back to the icy, distant girl I'd begun to know.

She didn't wait for me to get her door. She was out and around the car by the time I stepped out. We walked next to each other in silence. Her angry tension had morphed into relaxation. It was nice, not feeling like she would murder me if she got the chance.

When we got to the front door, I pulled it open. The

smell of bacon and pancakes wafted out. I inhaled, my stomach growling the moment the smell hit my senses.

"Oh my," she whispered as she slipped off her shoes. "That smells amazing."

I shut the door behind us and kicked my shoes to the side. "Gran never skimps when it comes to breakfast."

"It's the most important meal of the day." Gran's raspy voice grew near as she appeared in the doorway to the kitchen. "Bella Davenport," she said.

"Gran," Bella said as she rushed forward and wrapped her arms around my grandmother.

I stood there, watching their interaction. It seemed like they hadn't talked in a while. It made me wonder what Bella had been doing while I was gone. But then the image of her mother drunk in the back seat flashed in my mind. Bella had been busy.

"Come on, let's eat," I said as I passed by them and headed into the kitchen.

We busied ourselves loading our plates up with eggs, pancakes, and bacon. As we settled into our seats, Gran and Bella fell into conversation that sounded as easy as breathing.

They laughed and joked as Bella told her about school and soccer. I sat back, munching on my food. I occasionally interjected my thoughts, but really, I was satisfied just listening to their conversation.

Gran finally laughed as she grabbed her mug and pushed her chair out. "I can always depend on you to give me the dirt, Bella." She walked over to the coffee pot and filled her cup.

"There's a lot of it," Bella said as she set her fork down next to her plate and leaned back, stretching out her stomach. "This was amazing. I haven't had a home-cooked meal that wasn't ramen in a long time."

Gran was mid-sip when she raised her gaze up to meet Bella's. A silence fell around us as the weight of Bella's statement hung in the air. We all knew what she was talking about. And it hurt.

"Bella, sweetheart, I'm so—"

Bella held up her hand. "Let's not talk about it, okay?" she asked. She was studying the table so hard. Her jaw was clenching, and I could see that she was working through something.

I glanced up to see Gran studying her. A moment later, Gran glanced over at me, and I could see my sadness reflected in her gaze. We both knew the hurt that Bella was going through, and we both hated that she was suffering.

Bella glanced around until her gaze fell on the clock above the stove. "I should get going," she said as she pushed away from the table. "I'll be late for work if I don't."

I nodded and stood as well. Bella thanked Gran and made her way to the front door. As I slipped past, Gran reached out and grabbed my arm. "Hey," she said with her voice low.

I paused and glanced over at her. Gran's gaze was serious as she stared up at me. "Take care of that girl."

I furrowed my brow. "I will." Why would she question that? Bella and I had been friends. Gran had to know that I wouldn't do anything to hurt Bella.

Gran studied me and then nodded. "I know, I just felt like those words needed to be spoken."

I reached out and gave Gran a one-armed hug. "I hear you loud and clear," I said as I dropped a kiss on top of her head.

Gran patted my back. As I stepped out of the kitchen, I heard the faucet turn on and the clatter of dishes.

I slipped on my shoes as I digested Gran's words. She wanted me to protect Bella. To keep her safe.

I was going to do exactly that. The more time I spent around Bella, the more I began to realize that there was a very slim chance I was going to be able to walk away from her again.

Things were changing. I was beginning to doubt that we could go back to being friends. There was a very good chance that I wanted to be more.

CHAPTER NINE

Bella

The movie theater was quiet, which was expected for a Monday afternoon the week before school started. Everyone was at the pool, the Falls, or on a trip to the beach, leaving Sweet Mountain to feel like a ghost town. Which worked for me. It made my job easier.

I sighed as I leaned my arms on the counter in front of me. I was grateful for the lack of movie-goers. The solitude was giving me time to think. Time to digest what had happened this morning. When Logan showed up at my house.

He was nice. And kind. And patient. And all the things I had convinced myself he wasn't.

Nerves bubbled up inside of me so I pushed back and straightened up. I had four hours and fifteen minutes before I could leave for the day. Which felt like an eternity.

Needing to do something other than obsess about Logan, I grabbed a broom and began sweeping up the spilled popcorn on the floor.

That distracted me until I emptied the dustpan into the garbage and put the broom away.

Now I had only four hours to kill before I could leave. Before I could grab a soccer ball and release all of my tension on the field. Running would give my heart a reason to pound the wasn't the memory of Logan smiling down at me.

Falling for Logan Cartwright in any way, shape, or form was not going to happen. I was an idiot to even entertain those thoughts. Him being nice to me and feeding me breakfast was not a good enough reason for me to stop hating him.

The Cartwrights broke my family, and no matter how I looked at it, Logan was a Cartwright. It was in their DNA to hurt those close to them. In the end, I was going to be left holding my broken, hemorrhaging heart.

Noise at the front drew my attention, and I smiled as I saw Gigi walk in. She had giant sunglasses on and a flowy summer dress. She always looked so over-the-top but had a way of making it look amazing.

Someday, she was going to move to Hollywood and grace the movie screen with her beauty.

She must have spotted me, because she raised her

fingers and marched over to where I stood. "Bella, there you are."

I nodded as I rested my hands on the countertop in front of me. "Where else would I be?"

Gigi pulled her sunglasses off and gave me an incredulous look. "I stopped by your house this morning, but you weren't there." She narrowed her eyes. "Why weren't you there?"

I sighed as I played with some spilled salt. I pushed it around with my finger. There was no way I could tell Gigi that I'd been with Logan this morning. She would never understand, and she would never let me live it down.

"I had an errand to run this morning," I said in the calmest voice I could muster.

Gigi studied me with her eyes narrowed. "Is that so?"

I nodded. "Where else would I go?"

She folded her arms, her gaze not leaving my face. "So Logan Cartwright droping you off was...a figment of my imagination?"

My heart pounded, causing my cheeks to flush. Crap. What was I supposed to do with that? I hadn't expected her to see us.

Us? What was wrong with me?

"He was...I..." Nothing I could think of to justify us being together made sense. So, I sighed and decided to go with the truth. "His Gran invited me over for breakfast, so I went." I shrugged and busied myself with wiping the salt from the counter.

Gigi's hand shot out and grabbed mine. She squeezed so hard I feared I'd lose my fingers. "Logan Cartwright invited you over for breakfast?" she asked.

I sighed and looked up at her. "His grandma invited me over. That's all. We ate breakfast, and he took me home. I got dressed and came here," I said as I lifted my free hand to wave it around like I needed to remind her where we were.

I could tell from the way she was staring at me, Gigi didn't believe a word I said. So I shot her a hopefully confident smile. "Popcorn?" I asked as I turned away and grabbed one of our courtesy bags.

I didn't wait for her to answer. I filled the bag and handed it to her. She took it and began to munch on the pieces as she continued to stare me down. Finally, after what felt like an eternity under my best friend's scrutiny, she spoke.

"When do you get off?"

I was so relieved she wasn't going to drill me about Logan anymore, that I almost forgot her question. I shifted my weight and glanced down at the clock on the register in front of me. "At four."

She nodded as she continued to slip popcorn into her mouth. "Perfect. I'll pick you up at five. We're meeting at the Falls to hang out, and you're coming with me."

I parted my lips to complain. I didn't have the time or desire to go hang out with anyone tonight—much less a bunch of Gigi's friends who I didn't like and who didn't like me—but Gigi didn't wait to hear my excuses. Instead, she gave me a quick smile, slipped on her sunglasses, and headed out the front doors of the theater. I saw her yellow Bug drive by the big picture windows.

Thankfully, a few daycare groups showed up, and we were busy filling tiny trays with popcorn, soda, and treats for a good two hours. Then the evening rush of people started, and when I glanced up at the clock, it was time for me to go.

I waved at Tony, the assistant manager, as I grabbed my purse from behind the counter and slipped the strap over my shoulder. I pushed my hair from my face and strode across the foyer and out into the hot, sticky summer air.

Gigi texted me at least ten times between the theater and my house. I called her to tell her I was driving and if she wanted me as a friend forever, she needed to stop distracting me. She relented only when I agreed to be ready to go in two hours.

But as I stepped into my house, the desire to leave again left me. I groaned. I would be a horrible friend if I ditched Gigi.

After kicking off my shoes, I changed out of my uniform and into a pair of shorts and a t-shirt. I grabbed a frozen dinner, poked holes into the plastic wrap, and stuck it in the microwave.

With a Pepsi in hand, I grabbed my dinner and a fork and made my way into the living room to drown my day in

Korean dramas. I settled onto the couch and turned on the TV.

Two hours flew by fast, and before I knew it, my doorbell rang. I sighed as I pulled off my blanket and stood. Gigi didn't wait for me to open the door. She barged in—per usual.

She had on a long, lacy swimsuit cover and her hair was pulled up into a messy bun on the top of her head. Her sunglasses were still perched on her nose even though the sun was beginning to disappear behind the tips of the trees.

"Hey, Gigi," I said as I almost melted under her scrutiny. She slipped her glasses to the top of her head, folded her arms, and tapped her finger.

"Are you ready?" she asked.

I glanced down at my clothes. I gave her an apologetic smile and turned to head up the stairs. "Give me five."

I got dressed in my swimsuit and pulled on a loose t-shirt dress. I braided my hair and slipped on my flip-flops. Just as I went to open my bedroom door, my phone chimed. I sighed as I prepared myself for a text from Gigi telling me to hurry up, but when I glanced down, my heart began to pound. It wasn't a text from Gigi.

It was from Logan.

I swallowed the emotions that had risen up inside of me as I swiped my phone so I could read it.

Hey, just wondering if you were going to the Falls tonight.

I inhaled deeply as I read his words. Why did my stomach lighten at the thought of seeing him there? Why did I even care?

My defenses were down, that was for sure. Only an idiot would willingly let a person who broke their family into their life. Only an idiot would react like this to a text.

I mulled over what to say for a few seconds before I tapped the text bar and the keyboard showed up.

Gigi's dragging me along.

I sent that text off but then realized that I hadn't exactly answered his question, so I quickly typed out—*So yes, I'm going.*

My fingers hovered over the letters as I contemplated what to say next. Taking courage, I did something I never thought I would do.

You?

My stomach felt as if it would curl into a ball as I waited for his response. What was he thinking? Was I too eager? Should I have just let things be?

I groaned and tipped my face toward the ceiling. I closed my eyes and took in a few deep breaths. Something was definitely wrong with me. I needed to get a grip if I was going to survive tonight.

I needed to stop having whatever feelings I was having toward Logan. Nothing good ever came from trusting a Cartwright. Nothing good ever came from letting a Cartwright into your life.

Eventually, Logan was going to hurt me. Eventually,

he was going to break my heart. And the only person I'd have to blame was me.

Just as I began to gain some kind of control over myself, my phone chimed again. I glanced down to see Logan had messaged back. Like a dork, I clicked on the text before I allowed my brain to catch up.

I'm finding the motivation to go. I'll see you there?

My head clouded as I read his words. He was finding the motivation? Did that mean he didn't have motivation before he texted me? Did that mean he was going because I said I was?

I wrapped my arm around my stomach and sunk to the ground. I hated how conflicted I felt about all of this. Then it hit me. Why was it when I got even a glimmer of excitement about Logan, I felt as if I was betraying my parents?

Was it fair that they put this kind of pressure on me?

I let out a sigh as I stood and shoved my phone into my purse. Then I turned and opened the door and made my way down the stairs to where Gigi was waiting for me. She was on her phone and didn't acknowledge me until I was standing a few feet away from her.

"You look great," she said as she slipped her phone into the pocket of her cover-up and grabbed my hand. "Let's go."

I allowed her to drag me from my house and over to her car. Once we were inside and buckled, she started the engine and pulled out of my driveway.

She filled the drive with chatter. She told me about

school and what outfit she was planning for the first day. I nodded along with her and offered her short affirmations, all the while keeping my arm wrapped around my stomach and my gaze out the window.

While she talked, I thought about Logan and what I was going to do when I got there.

By the time we pulled into the parking lot at the base of the trail that led to the Falls, my mind was a muddled mess. Nothing was making sense anymore. Logan had successfully found the chink in my armor and was slowly whittling it down to nothing.

I was scared to see him again, but at the same time, I was excited. I hated that I had such polarizing emotions about a Cartwright. When he wasn't around, incessantly trying to insert himself into my life, I was okay. I could hate him with as much passion as I could muster. Everything made sense when he wasn't around me, contradicting what I'd previously assumed to be true.

But him being here and being a part of my life was throwing my entire system out of whack.

"Let's go," Gigi said as she pulled on her door handle and stepped out of the car.

I nodded and followed her order. Right now, it seemed wise to just act. With Gigi around, I could rely on her to direct me. Most of the time. I, on the other hand, always ended up making the wrong choice.

Case in point: my sudden desire to spend a lot of time around Logan.

RULE #11: YOU CAN'T IGNORE YOUR FAMILY FEUD

Hopefully, at the Falls, Gigi would stick by my side and not let me go. Because if she did, and Logan found me, I feared what I might do. With the way I was feeling, there was a good chance I would let the rest of my walls down and let Logan in fully.

And my head knew that would be a major mistake. If only my heart would get on board, then I'd be okay.

CHAPTER TEN

Logan

Was it weird that I kept looking for Bella? Every time someone approached our group, I basically broke my back trying to see if it was Bella.

Which was ridiculous. We'd only been back in each other's lives for a few short days. But there was something about being around her again and remembering what our friendship used to be like that made it feel like we were picking up where we'd left off—only better.

By the time I heard her voice and glanced over to see her approach with Gigi, I felt as if I was going to go into cardiac arrest. She looked beautiful in her dark green dress with her hair pulled back. Wispy curls framed her face, and when her gaze met mine, I swear, my entire nervous system short-circuited.

The sides of her lips tipped up into a smile, and suddenly, I was walking across the grass to greet her. Not sure what I was going to do when I got there, I pushed my hands through my hair and grinned down at her.

I grinned. Like an idiot.

"Hey, Bella," I said.

She looked up at me with her eyes wide and then dropped her gaze and nodded. "Hey, Logan."

An awkward silence fell around us, and I cursed myself for turning into a bumbling idiot. I was a confident guy. Why was I acting like I'd never spoken to a girl before?

This was just Bella.

Right. This was Bella. Things were different.

Not wanting to make her uncomfortable, I reached out and brushed her elbow with my fingertips. It had been an instinctive move, but as soon as I felt her tense up, I worried I'd gone too far. So I pulled back and nodded toward the drink table.

"Can I get you something?"

Bella glanced over her shoulder and nodded. "Yeah, sure. A water would be great."

I smiled and winked—and then shot her an apologetic look. "Sorry, habit."

The red hue that flushed her cheeks caused my heart to pound faster. She shrugged and said, "I'm getting used to it." Then she turned and started talking to Gigi.

I nodded and made my way through the crowd and

over to the table. Miller was standing there, chatting with some other guys I used to hang out with. We greeted each other with a hand shake and bro-hug. I didn't want to get distracted, so I quickly ended our conversation and grabbed a water bottle.

My phone buzzed, and I reached down to grab it from my pocket. As soon as I saw *Dad* on the screen, my stomach sank. Whatever he wanted to say to me, I didn't want to hear. The last thing I wanted to do when I was attempting to hang out with Bella, was talk to the people that broke her heart. Broke her family.

Turning my phone off, I slipped it back into my pocket and raised my gaze in search of Bella. I was making progress with gaining her trust, and I wasn't about to let that go. Whatever Dad had to say, it could wait.

I found Bella near the waterfall. She was sitting on a rock, staring down into the water. I moved to stand behind her, but then, feeling like a creeper, I sat down next to her.

She must have not noticed me, because when my arm brushed hers, she jumped and shifted to face me. She studied me for a moment before she settled down and wrapped her fingers around her upper arms.

"Here," I said, offering her the water bottle.

Bella hesitated before she took it from me, cracked the top open, and took a drink. When she was finished, she twisted the cap on and set the bottle on the ground next to her.

RULE #11: YOU CAN'T IGNORE YOUR FAMILY FEUD   101

The air around us fell silent as we both sat there, staring at the water rushing down in front of us. The noise drowned out the party going on behind us. And for the first time in a long time, I felt at peace.

And I never in a million years would have thought that would be possible. At least, not in Bella's presence.

"Have a good day at work?" I asked as I peered over at her.

Bella didn't respond right away. Instead, she squinted as she focused on the scenery. "Yeah. It was uneventful."

I nodded. "That's good. Better than busy."

Bella nodded slowly and then tightened her arms around her stomach.

I could feel her beginning to pull back, so I shifted until I was facing her. I wanted to be back in her life. I missed being around her. And I needed to tell her that.

"How's your mom?" I traced my finger along the grooves in the rock as I waited, hoping I hadn't overstepped. I already knew her secret, and I wanted to help her. She had to know that.

Bella dropped her gaze to her lap and pinched her lips together. Then she sighed and glanced over at me. "She's doing better. She actually went to work today." She studied me for a moment, then returned her focus to her lap.

"That's good." I found myself leaning in to Bella. There was this deep desire I had to fix her. To mend her broken heart. Despite her determination to keep people at arm's length, I knew what she was hiding. That she was hurting.

"How long has it been like this?" My voice dropped an octave, both out of fear and concern. How was I going to deal with the fact that she was broken because of my family? Because of me.

I peeked over at her and had to blink a few times before I registered what I was seeing.

A tear was rolling down her cheek. Bella's eyes were closed, her lips pinched, as she sat there completely still. Her sadness surrounded me, and I found myself reaching out to brush the tear from her cheek. My fingertips lingered on her skin as I studied her.

Everything around me began to fade away as we sat there. Bella didn't speak as she tipped her head to the side and met my gaze. Her eyes were red, and she sniffled.

"I'm so sorry," I whispered.

Her brow furrowed as she stared at me. It felt like an eternity passed by before she moved. Then, suddenly, she stood and slipped off her swimsuit cover. Confused, I watched as she set her dress on the rock and kicked off her sandals.

She walked over to the edge of the falls and dove into the water below.

I sat there, stunned, as I watched her disappear. It took a few seconds for me to react. I slipped off my shirt and set it behind me. Then I pulled out my phone and removed my shoes. There was no way I was letting her get away.

My stomach left my body as I dove off the side, and the chill slammed into me as I sliced through the water. I flipped my body up and kicked my feet until I broke the surface.

After scanning around me, I found Bella bobbing a few feet away. She looked beautiful as the moon reflected off the water's surface and illuminated her skin.

She was staring at me, and for the first time, I felt completely exposed. Like she was seeing into my soul. I lowered my defenses and swam over to her until we were inches away.

"That was...drastic," I said in a playful voice as I winked at her.

She didn't move her gaze away from my face. She just stayed there, watching me. "Why do you suddenly care so much about me and my life?" she finally asked.

My hands moved in the water as I kicked to keep myself afloat. I was grateful for the distraction that gave me. She wanted me to be honest? I'd be honest.

"Bella, I never stopped caring."

My words must have shocked her because she stopped moving. She took in a deep breath and slipped under the water. I pushed up so I could attempt to see through the dark water. Just when I began to worry that she wasn't going to come back up, she surfaced...inches away from me.

Out of instinct, I gripped her upper arms to keep her from going back under. Her eyes widened, and water glistened off her eyelashes and skin. The color of her lips darkened, and her cheeks flushed.

"Why?" she asked. I wasn't sure, but it looked as if new tears had formed on her eyelids.

"We were friends once. Before all of this with our parents. I never wanted to give that up. Not for anything. I guess I was just an idiot who went along with a horrible plan." I pulled her close to me. The only thing I wanted to do was hug her. To feel her body pressed against mine.

"Logan," she whispered. I saw fear and worry flash in her gaze, and it killed me to think that she was worried about what I was going to do to her. That she thought I was here to break her more than she already was.

Wanting to give her space, I let her float away from me. Not too far, though. I needed to keep her near. She was a calm in the storm of my mind. My heart.

"You don't think we can move on from this?" I asked as I floated near her. I wanted to give her space, but I didn't want her to climb back into the cave of her pain. She'd come out for a brief moment, and I wanted to find a way to keep her here.

She studied me, and I couldn't help but revel in her beauty. Her wide eyes and the way she kept chewing her bottom lip had my head spinning and my heart hammering.

All I wanted to do was pull her close and kiss her.

Without thinking, I lifted my hand up to her forehead and pushed back her hair, tucking it behind her ears. I heard her suck in her breath. I saw her eyes widen, and for a moment, I allowed myself to believe that she leaned into my touch.

Was that possible?

"I'm not sure if I can trust you," she whispered. A soft sob escaped her lips as she dropped her gaze and blinked as if she were trying to dispel tears.

I held her gaze and moved closer to her. How was I going to get her to trust that what I said was true? That I cared about her. And that, from this moment on, I wasn't going to let my family hurt her anymore.

My gaze fell to her lips, and I was filled with the urge to show her. So I pushed out all my doubts and pulled her to my chest. Then, with my hand on her cheek, I dipped down and brushed my lips against hers.

I rested there for a moment, waiting for her to do something—anything.

But she didn't. Worried I'd shocked her into confusion, I started to pull away, only to have her hands fly up to my neck and pull me back to her lips.

It was my turn to be stunned. But that only lasted for a moment as I took note of her body, her hands, her lips. They were all pressed to me, igniting a fire inside of me.

My hands found her waist, and I pulled her against me, wrapping my arms around her. I wasn't going to let her go.

Her lips moved against mine with a rhythm that felt familiar. I never imagined kissing Bella would feel this good, and now, I wasn't sure how I would ever feel satisfied with anyone else.

Eventually, I had to pull away, but not too far. I tipped my forehead and rested it against hers. Our breathing matched as we floated in the water with our arms wrapped around each other.

When she pulled back and looked up at me, my heart broke inside. Her cheeks were wet with tears as she searched my gaze, as if she were looking for answers. I wanted to give them to her.

I gently reached up and wiped her tears from her cheeks. "You can trust me," I said softly.

Her begging gaze met mine, and a surge of desire to protect her raced through me. I leaned forward and kissed each cheek. Then I found her hand and brought it out of the water to press my lips to it.

"I'm not going to hurt you. And I'm not going to go anywhere," I murmured.

When I brought my gaze back to meet Bella's, she had her lips pinched together. Suddenly, she surrounded me with both arms and pulled her body close to mine. I held her, one hand on her head and one around her waist as we hugged.

This was where I wanted to be. Wrapped up in Bella's arms. Both of our parents were losers. Both sets were ridiculous. But as long as I had Bella, I felt as if I could get through anything.

It took fighting parents and a family feud for me to realize just who I wanted in my corner. She was the girl I'd almost lost, and I wasn't going to let her go. Never again.

I was here to stay. I'd prove it to Bella.

I wasn't going anywhere.

CHAPTER ELEVEN

Bella

Was it possible to feel this happy?

Was I this lucky?

I'd spent so much of the past year hating Logan, and I'd convinced myself that I was happy. But I was naive and a fool. That wasn't happiness. This—sitting on a rock, wrapped in his arms, while we dried off—was happiness.

I never wanted it to end. I never wanted him to leave me again.

Mom and Dad had their issues, that was a fact. But it didn't matter to me anymore. I wasn't going to live my life for them. Especially not when it came to Logan.

For this moment I was happy, and I was going to bask in that happiness for as long as it lasted. Because I knew

RULE #11: YOU CAN'T IGNORE YOUR FAMILY FEUD

the moment we returned to real life, nothing was going to seem simple or straightforward.

"Okay, this is an unexpected twist." Gigi's voice drew my attention. She was standing next to us like a Greek goddess, staring down at our entwined fingers and Logan's arm wrapped securely around my shoulders.

I snuggled in closer to Logan. His warmth helped stave off the shivers that threatened as the breeze hit my wet skin. "Yeah," I said, giving her a sly smile. She grinned back and gave me a wink.

"I have to say, I've been rooting for you two to get together." She walked over and leaned down to give me a kiss on my cheek.

I gave her a quick hug and then settled back into Logan's embrace.

Gigi didn't stick around for long. As soon as someone called her name, she said goodbye and left, leaving Logan and me alone.

"Are you hungry?" he asked. His voice was low and filled with emotion that raised goosebumps on my skin.

I twisted to meet his gaze and smiled. "I could eat."

He nodded and began to pull away, but I reached out and pulled him back closer to me. "But I don't want you to go," I said.

Maybe it was fear that if he left, he would leave for good. Or perhaps, if he walked away, he'd realize that he made a mistake. If the choice was between eating or keeping Logan, I was going to go with keeping Logan.

He stopped moving and settled back in next to me. "Bella," he said with a flirty hint to his voice.

I studied my hands in my lap for a few seconds before I turned to face him. His brows were furrowed, but there was a sweet smile on his lips that made my stomach lighten. He reached up and tucked my hair behind my ear.

"I'll be right back." His fingertips lingered on my cheek as he met my gaze. Then he leaned forward and brushed his lips against mine. "I promise," he said as he leaned his forehead forward and rested it against mine.

I don't know why, but his words made me tear up. I had to stifle a sob as I nodded. I wasn't going to be the weak one. "Okay," I whispered.

He pressed his lips to my forehead and then reached out and squeezed my hands as he moved to stand. He held onto my fingers until the last minute, and then he disappeared over to the food table.

I sat there with my arms wrapped around my chest as I moved my focus to the ground. My mind was reeling from the events of the day. Logan had kissed me. And not only had he kissed me, but I'd kissed him back. My heart felt as if all the cracks were slowly healing.

All because of Logan.

A rush of fear pulsed through my body. What did that mean for us? For me? I wanted to trust him wholeheartedly. But, sitting here with the reality of what happened between us, I wasn't sure if I could.

What was I going to do when he decided he was done

with Sweet Mountain and wanted to leave? What was I going to do when he decided that being with me wasn't enough and he missed his cushy life in New York?

What was I going to do when Dad found out that I liked a Cartwright?

I blinked a few times as tears formed on my lids. I hated how messed up this all was. Most girls would be excited about their new relationship. They would be planning the next steps. They wouldn't be fearing what the future would bring.

I leaned forward on my elbows and sighed as I tipped my head forward and allowed my shoulders to slump. I took in some deep breaths then bit my bottom lip. I feared what I was going to do with these rising feelings. The last thing I wanted to do was ruin what had just barely begun.

I liked Logan, and Logan liked me. And really, that was all that mattered.

Thankfully, Logan returned before I spiraled any more. As soon as he sat down next to me, I reached out and pulled him in for a hug. He was gone for only five minutes, and yet during that time, I'd basically lost my mind.

He chuckled as he squeezed me back. He buried his face into my shoulder and took in a deep breath. We sat there, holding each other until catcalls and whistles pulled us apart. Logan chuckled as he handed the food over to me.

Thankfully, I felt as if I had better control over my

emotions and wasn't about to lose my crap. Plus, I was starving.

We spent the rest of the evening next to each other. Eventually, we got up and socialized, but I made sure Logan stuck by my side, which he didn't seem to mind. He kept his arm wrapped protectively around my waist.

I couldn't help but smile as I allowed my heart to swell, watching him talk to Trenton but keeping me pressed against his side. It was almost as if he wanted me as close to him as I wanted to remain.

The idea that Logan could like me as much as I was finding I liked him, made butterflies swarm my stomach. The idea that perhaps, in this crappy world, I could actually have a happy ending, made tears form on my lids.

I never thought I could be this happy, and now that I was, I feared what would happen to me if it ended. The nice thing about staying on the ground, the fall wasn't too far. But taking chances and climbing the mountain meant you had farther to fall.

And the farther you fell, the more it would hurt.

Logan must have sensed my worry. A moment later, he turned to me and pressed his lips against my temple. I glanced over at him, and he winked at me. I held his gaze for a moment before I smiled and nodded.

I didn't allow myself to spiral the rest of the night. I was going to enjoy what was happening and not let my fear cloud my happiness.

The night drew to a close, and Gigi met up with us.

RULE #11: YOU CAN'T IGNORE YOUR FAMILY FEUD 113

Her gaze roamed over us and finally landed on my face. She gave me a wide smile as she pulled me into her arms.

"I'm so happy for you," she said as she gave me a big squeeze.

I pulled back and furrowed my brow. "Thanks."

She nodded. "You deserve it. You've been so unhappy for so long. It's good to see you smile again."

A rush of emotions filled my chest and caused my throat to close up. I hated that I'd allowed my parents to run my life. That I allowed their mistakes to determine my happiness.

I didn't deserve what they'd done to me. They were adults, and yet they were acting like children. Running away or drowning themselves in a lifestyle that would never bring them the happiness they wanted.

I was going to live for me and my happiness. At least, when Logan was around. I feared who I would become when he was gone. I feared that I wouldn't be strong enough to be the person that he needed me to be.

Logan must have felt my change in emotions. He wrapped his arm around my waist and pulled me toward him. "I'm gonna get her home," he said to Gigi. She just nodded, not wanting to put up a fight, which I appreciated.

"Yes, sir," she said with a salute and a wink.

I grinned over my shoulder as Logan led me from the group and down the path to his car. He stopped outside of the passenger door and pulled it open.

I climbed in, and after I was situated, he shut the door and jogged around the hood to the driver's seat. He shut his door and looked over at me with a goofy smile I'd never really seen on him before.

He looked...happy. And it thrilled me to think that I had a hand in his joy.

I grinned back at him, and suddenly, he brought his arm around and leaned in toward me. My heart fluttered as I watched his face grow closer. My gaze instantly fell to his lips, and there was nothing I wanted more in this world than to feel them against my own.

But he pulled away and held out my seatbelt.

"Can't have you getting hurt. Especially since you just started liking me again." His words ended with the clicking sound of the buckle in its latch. I blinked a few times, enjoying the feeling of emotions that pulsed through me with every heartbeat.

As we pulled out of the parking lot, I glanced over at him. I wanted to say something, but I just wasn't sure how. I wanted him to know that I was sorry for the way I'd treated him. It wasn't fair that I blamed him for something that wasn't in his control.

He deserved better than what I'd given him.

He got onto the freeway, and just as he settled back with his wrist resting on the steering wheel, I turned to him. He didn't meet my gaze. Instead, his jaw twitched as he kept his attention on the road in front of us.

I studied him, loving the way his profile looked. I'd

never thought I could feel this happy again, and yet, here I was, caring for the one guy I thought I'd hate for my entire life.

Logan's free hand reached out and engulfed my own. He squeezed it as he leaned over, all the while not taking his eye off the road. "You're going to melt me into a pile of goo," he said, ending with another squeeze of my hand.

I smiled as my cheeks heated, and I dropped my gaze. I reached out and covered his hand with my free one. "Sorry," I whispered.

Logan chuckled and shook his head. "I'm not complaining. It's just distracting me. And the last thing I would do is hurt you once more." His words drifted off as if they hurt to say.

Which made me sad. I didn't want him to feel like that. It wasn't his fault. What happened between our families wasn't his fault any more than it was mine.

"I don't blame you," I said, my throat constricting from the feelings coursing through me.

He paused, and I felt his gaze on me. "You don't?"

I shook my head as a tear slipped down my cheek. I hated that I cried this much around him. But I was beginning to realize that it was part of my healing process. I had so much anger and hurt built up inside of me, and the only way to move on was to cry it out. How else would I release it all?

"You need to stop crying," he said gently as he reached over and wiped away my tear.

Feeling like an idiot, I swallowed and nodded, trying with all my might to push down my broken heart and be stronger. "I'm sorry."

Logan's fingers lingered on my cheek before they dropped back down to my hand.

"It's not like that. I don't mind you crying. It just makes me want to murder whoever hurt you. It breaks my heart that I can't do anything to take your pain. And that's all I want to do." I raised my eyes to meet his gaze. He smiled softly before he turned his attention back to the road. "I want to fix everything that is hurting you," he said as he brought his hand to the steering wheel.

I smiled. I wanted to smile. I wanted to feel hopeful. Logan had given that to me.

"Thanks," I said as I shifted my weight so that I could lean over the center console. As soon as my head touched his shoulder, my entire body relaxed.

And that was how we drove home. My head on his shoulder, and his focus on the road. Occasionally, he would reach over and rest his hand on my knee, and every time he took it away to turn the steering wheel, I wanted to pull it back.

He made me feel safe. He made me feel at home.

Whatever was going to happen in the future was going to happen. For now, I was going to be happy.

I deserved it.

CHAPTER TWELVE

Logan

It was hard walking away from Bella after I dropped her off at her house. She looked so small and frail as she walked into her house, leaving me on her doorstep. But she assured me that she was going to be okay.

And that she wanted to see me first thing tomorrow.

I stood there for a few seconds, staring at her closed front door, before I forced myself to walk down the stairs and climb into my car. I started my engine and drove away.

The entire ride home, I couldn't stop the smile on my lips. I must have looked like the Joker. But I couldn't help it.

I was unbelievably happy.

Bella made me happy. And the fact that she trusted

me made me want to live to keep her trust. I would be the one person in her life that she could guarantee wouldn't hurt her or leave her. I would be the knight she was waiting for.

Nothing was going to deter me. I wasn't going anywhere ever again.

I pulled into Gran's driveway and turned off the car. As I got out, I grabbed my stuff from the back and then slammed the driver's door closed. I fished my phone out of my pocket and glanced down at the black screen. Right. I'd turned it off.

I quietly opened the back door as I held down my phone's power button. The kitchen light was on. Gran didn't normally stay awake this late so it completely surprised me when I found her sitting at her table, sipping what I could only assume was some bourbon in her fancy glass.

"Hey," I said as I kicked off my shoes. All the waterfall water had dried on my skin, and I was ready to take a hot shower and crawl into bed. The sooner I went to bed, the sooner I was going to see Bella.

Gran cleared her throat and glanced over at me. "Where did you go?"

I sighed as I collapsed on a chair across from her. I leaned back and let my legs and arms fall naturally. Was it possible for someone to feel so completely at peace? Because that was how I felt right now. Completely and wholly at peace.

RULE #11: YOU CAN'T IGNORE YOUR FAMILY FEUD

"At the Falls with some friends...and Bella." My cheeks flushed at the feeling of her name on my tongue. It felt great, being honest and open about my feelings for her.

I didn't have to hide anything anymore. She cared about me, and I cared about her. And really, that was all I needed.

The sound of Gran's glass thudding on the table drew my attention over to her. Her brow was furrowed as she studied me. "Did you talk to your father?"

I cleared my throat as the sense of completeness left my body in a whoosh. I straightened and rested my elbows on the table. "No. What's up?"

Gran shifted her weight. "He called. They found an investor." She raised her gaze to meet mine.

I shrugged. "It has nothing to do with me. I'm here now."

Gran sighed, and from that one sound, my entire body went numb. "You're moving to Italy. Apparently, the investors want your father where they can see him." She pushed away from the table and headed over to the sink, where she turned on the water and began to rinse out her glass.

My ears rang as I sat there, staring at her. Was she serious? "Gran, you're kicking me out?" I asked as I stumbled to my feet.

Gran sighed again, then turned off the water and turned to face me. "You belong with your parents, seeing the world. This is a small town. People come and go. But those who stay..." She swallowed. "They don't leave. And you deserve a lot more than what Sweet Mountain has to offer."

I approached her with my hand extended. "I want to stay here, though. With you...with Bella." My stomach felt as if she'd just gut-punched me. I ached everywhere.

What an awful, evil joke my parents were playing on me. Dumping me back in our hometown only to drag me away a week later. What did they think would happen? That I would just willingly go with them? I didn't want to move to Italy. I was happy with my life here.

Gran's hand reached out and grabbed mine. I raised my gaze up to see her earnest eyes. "I know if feels as if you can't leave, but it gets easier. I promise you. You'll be grateful that you left." She reached out and patted my cheek with her hand. "If Bella cares about you like it seems she does, she'll understand too."

I stepped back, breaking Gran's hold on me. I didn't want to hear what she had to say. She was wrong. Bella wouldn't understand, and I wouldn't be grateful. I wanted to stay here, at least until graduation; then I would run off to college with Bella.

She was the life I wanted. Not my parents' idea of a perfect life. Of a perfect future where they screwed over people to get rich. How could I face them after falling for Bella?

How could I face Bella?

"I can't go," I said. I sounded desperate, but I didn't

care. Gran had to see that what she was asking me wasn't right. How could she ask me to leave? To walk away from the life I was trying to create here.

Gran studied me for a moment before she sighed and sidestepped me. "I need to lie down. I'll see you in the morning."

I watched as she shuffled across the room and over to the stairs. Once she disappeared, I leaned against the counter and folded my arms. I closed my eyes as I imagined what Bella would do with my news. What would she say?

I could only imagine how broken her expression would be. I growled and stomped over to the cupboard for a glass. I downed a cup of water, but the cool temperature did nothing for my anger.

Frustrated, I set the glass down on the counter and made my way to my room and collapsed on my bed. I covered my face with arm and took in a few deep breaths.

Determination grew inside of me as I pulled my arm away and stared up the ceiling. Dad could say whatever he wanted. I wasn't going to go anywhere. He was the one who'd moved me back here. Who was he to think that he could control my life?

I wasn't his butler or his employee, so he didn't get to dictate where I went. He certainly wasn't going to drag me from the one place that had always felt like home to me. He wasn't going to drag me from the place where I belonged.

After a long shower, I climbed into bed and flipped off the light. I needed to think of something to distract myself from the storm coming. A smile crept over my lips as I thought of Bella and the night we spent together. I could still feel her lips against mine and see the way she looked up at me.

My stomach lightened as I flopped over and closed my eyes. I was excited to sleep because I was excited to wake up tomorrow. I was going to spend the entire day with Bella. And not only that, I was going to spend my senior year with her as well.

The days of my parents running my life was over.

I was going to take over from now on.

THE SUN STREAMED through my blinds and right into my eyes. At first, I was frustrated, but then Bella's face flashed in my mind and I threw off my covers. We were going to meet up before the car wash we had to host today, and I couldn't wait to spend my entire day with her.

I dressed and walked out into the kitchen to find Gran sitting at the table with a coffee in hand and the newspaper spread out in front of her. She glanced up at me and grunted. I nodded and winked as I grabbed my keys and headed to the back door.

She could say—or not say—what she wanted. I was staying here. Period.

RULE #11: YOU CAN'T IGNORE YOUR FAMILY FEUD

Just as I moved to pull the door shut, Gran's voice stopped me in my tracks. "Your parents are going to be here later tonight. Be ready," she said.

I paused as anger and frustration rushed through me. I thought about replying, but decided against it. I wasn't going, so there was no use in arguing.

I'd listened to Dad's many voicemails this morning. I knew he was excited. The prospect of not losing the company that he'd worked so hard to steal from Bella's dad had brightened his mood. He suddenly sounded like the dad he should've been all along.

But his happiness meant nothing when Bella's family was in shambles. I purposely didn't call him back. I didn't want to speak to him. He couldn't just drop people when he didn't need them only to pull them back when things were going well.

I wasn't going to go through that emotional whiplash any longer. I was done being a Cartwright.

But I didn't want to be disrespectful to my grandmother, so I nodded in acknowledgment and then shut the door behind me. I jogged down the stairs and over to my car.

It took exactly ten minutes to get to Bella's house. I couldn't help the smile that emerged as I pulled my keys from the ignition and climbed out. I didn't try to hide my excitement as I hurried across her front yard and up to her door.

I knocked a few times and waited, peeking up at the

windows on the second story. Was she home? A nervous feeling built up inside of me as I bounced from my heels to my toes.

Had I imagined yesterday? Had it really happened?

Just as I was beginning to dive into a spiral of self-doubt, the front door opened, and Bella stood on the other side. I held my breath as I searched her face. For some reason, I was anticipating the same expression she'd showed me yesterday when I picked her up for breakfast.

Her gaze rose to meet mine, and to my relief, she smiled as she stepped out onto the stairs and pulled me into a hug.

"Hi," she whispered as she pulled back to stare up at me.

I studied her, just to make sure that this was real. Then I cupped the back of her head with my hand and pulled her back in, crushing her to my chest.

"Hey," I said. I leaned forward and nuzzled the spot between her neck and shoulder.

She giggled as she tipped her head back and tightened her arms around me. I kissed a trail of kisses from her neck, to her ear, and then ended at her lips.

This was where I belonged. Not in Italy trying to live my parents' idea of happiness.

I belonged right here. With Bella.

She giggled and pulled me closer. I took in a deep breath, trying to memorize the feeling of her body against

RULE #11: YOU CAN'T IGNORE YOUR FAMILY FEUD

mine. I didn't want to let any of this go. She was mine, and I was going to fight to keep her.

But we couldn't stand on her stoop, holding each other for the rest of our lives. And if I kept acting like this, Bella was going to wonder what was wrong with me.

So I pulled back and glanced down at her. "Ready?" I asked.

She furrowed her brow. "For what?"

I wrapped my hand around hers and headed down her front steps. "To spend the day with me," I said as I pulled her next to me.

She laughed and fell into step. "Of course."

As we approached my car, I felt Bella tighten next to me. The air felt cold, and I glanced over to see her face was as white as a sheet. Her lips were parted, and her eyes were wide as she stared at a black car that was approaching her house.

I squinted as I tried to see into the driver's side.

"Dad?" Bella whispered, and my entire body felt numb.

"Dad?" I asked, staring down at her.

Bella broke away from me and started walking toward the car that was now pulled up in front of the garage door. "Dad?" Bella asked again, this time louder.

The driver's door swung open and Mr. Davenport stepped out. His hair was disheveled, as were his clothes. I almost didn't recognize him behind his straggly hair and beard. His gaze landed on me, and he narrowed his eyes.

"What are you doing here?" he bellowed. Suddenly, he lunged at me, but he must have been drinking, because he staggered to the left and to the right before he bent over.

"Dad," Bella screamed. She had tears running down her cheeks, and she rushed over to Mr. Davenport and wrapped her arm around his shoulders. "What are you doing?" she asked.

Mr. Davenport straightened and swung his arm to push her away. "How could you bring him around here?" he asked. His tone was bitter, and it caused rage to rise up inside of me.

Worried for Bella, I made my way over to stand between them. I wasn't going to let him hurt her, and from the look on his face, he was going to try.

"I think you should go inside," I said as I lowered my voice. He was going to take me seriously if it killed me. Bella was mine to protect now, even if that meant protecting her from her father.

Mr. Davenport stared at me before he slowly began to stand. His brow was furrowed as he glared at me. "You're just a good-for-nothing Cartwright. Get off my property," he said as she straightened and raised his fist.

There was a crack, and suddenly, I was seeing sparks. I staggered backwards, my hand flying to my cheek as a pulsing pain shot through my face.

I heard Bella scream, but the blow from Mr. Davenport was affecting my hearing. She sounded far away

RULE #11: YOU CAN'T IGNORE YOUR FAMILY FEUD

even though I could feel her hands wrapped around my arm.

"Dad, what are you doing?" she cried. I blinked a few times, trying to regain my bearings.

"Get off my property!" Mr. Davenport yelled.

I raised my hand as my sight returned. But before I could respond, Bella leaned in. "Please, go," she whispered.

I peered down at her to see her wide eyes and tears streaming down her cheeks. "But, Bella—"

"You need to go," she said again, this time with more force. And suddenly, her hands were on my back, shoving me in the direction of my car.

"I can't just leave you here," I said as I turned around and grabbed her hands. If something happened to her, I'd never forgive myself. I couldn't just turn my back on her.

She stared up at me for a moment before dropping her gaze down to our clasped hands. Then she shook her head. "I'll be fine. Don't worry about me," she whispered.

I could hear Mr. Davenport cursing, and from the corner of my eye, I could see him lumbering toward us. He was going to keep coming if I didn't leave.

So I squeezed Bella's hands once more. "Call me," I whispered before I hurried over to my car.

I didn't stop until I was pulling my car around the corner and out of view. I threw the car into park and gripped the steering wheel as I closed my eyes. My adrenaline was dissipating, and I felt as if I'd run a marathon.

Anger burned in my stomach as I cursed and pounded my hands on the steering wheel. I wanted to go back. I wanted to grab Bella and take her away with me, to leave our parents to figure out their own revenge.

It wasn't fair to drag us all through the mud because they were selfish.

I closed my eyes and tipped my head back to rest on the seat. I took in a few deep breaths as I willed myself to calm down.

My phone chimed, and I didn't hesitate to grab it and look down at the screen.

I'm okay, but I won't be there for the car wash. You'll have to do it without me.

My heart pounded as I hurried to respond. *Should I come get you?*

I waited and waited for her response, but nothing came. Right before I was about to go insane with waiting, my phone chimed again.

Goodbye, Logan.

I stared at her final words, my brain trying to figure out what she meant.

Goodbye? Was she leaving? What was happening?

I threw my phone onto the passenger seat and started the engine. I drove by her house about a thousand times, but I never saw her, and she didn't text me again.

Her house remained dark, with the drapes drawn. It was like a ghost house.

When I finally resigned myself to the fact that she

wasn't coming out or calling me, I drove back to Gran's house. I swallowed hard as I tried to keep my emotions in check. Even if Bella said goodbye, that didn't mean what we had was over.

I was going to fight for her.

CHAPTER THIRTEEN

Bella

Dad was angry. Mom was angry. *I* was angry.

Nothing they were saying made any sense. They'd sat me down and were staring at me from the other couch, which made me even angrier. They had their arms folded and scowls on their faces that I could only assume matched my own.

Why were they mad? They had nothing to be angry about. Logan had nothing to do with his parents' betrayal. He was nothing like the Cartwrights—nothing like my parents.

Dad sighed and crossed his legs. "Bella, you shouldn't be running around with that boy," he said.

My eyes widened. Was he serious? "What do you

care? You're never around. Always off doing who-knows-what with who-knows-who." I glowered at him as I folded my arms across my chest.

"Bella," Mom said. She had a wineglass sandwiched between her fingers, and she was nursing the wine inside of it. Picture of parenthood, people.

I sighed and shifted in my seat. I didn't want to sit around here, listening to my parents talk about my poor judgment. Being with Logan was the best decision I'd made in a long time. It felt corny and ridiculous to say, but he completed me in a way I didn't think was possible.

"You can't control my life like this," I said as I steeled my gaze.

Mom's eyebrows rose as she studied me, then she shifted her attention over to Dad who was working his jaw muscles.

I met his gaze with as much force as he was giving to me. He wasn't going to intimidate me. I was going to hold my ground. I was tired of living in the past. I was tired of being angry just to be angry.

They were the adults in this situation, and yet they were doing anything but being adults.

"Bella," Dad said as he stood and made his way over to the front windows. He shoved his hands into his front pockets and stared outside.

"Dad, it's time to move on," I said as I shifted in my seat so I could face him. "What happened, happened. Can we just let it go?" I'd spent most nights pretending that I didn't want to be the same old family we used to be growing up. I'd tried to convince myself that I didn't want my old parents back.

But I knew that was far from the truth. I missed Dad. I missed Mom. I missed what we used to be as a family.

But if they were asking me to pick between them and Logan, here and now? I was picking Logan. Every time.

Logan was going to stick around. My parents were content to drown their sorrows in whatever felt good at the moment. They were always going to pick nursing their wounds over me. They weren't doing anything to fix the things in their lives that were hurting them. They were allowing the injury caused by the Cartwrights to fester.

They were willing to give up on their family—to hurt their daughter—all in the name of their ridiculous grudge. They couldn't see that Logan was good for me. That I was finally happy for the first time in a long time.

Which was why I wasn't going to be loyal to them anymore.

I had someone else in my life who cared about me. I felt seen. I felt heard. And there was no other place I wanted to be than with Logan.

I wiped my tears and stood. I grabbed my purse, and before Mom could ask what I was doing, I was out the front door. I didn't bother to tell them where I was going. After all, isn't that how we handled things in this family? Leaving without a word. Doing what we wanted no matter how it affected others. It was what they did. Why would they expect anything different from me?

I felt as if I held my breath the entire drive to Logan's house. By the time I pulled into the driveway, I was sobbing. Tears were flowing freely. I was so broken, I was beginning to doubt my ability to put myself back together.

I needed to see Logan. He would know what to do.

He knew what it was like to be disappointed by your family. He knew my secrets.

I didn't even bother to grab my purse as I pulled my keys from the ignition and threw them on the passenger seat. I pulled on the door handle and stepped out, slamming the door behind me.

I attempted to get ahold of my emotions as I made my way to the back of the house. I'd try to find Logan there. With the way I was feeling, I didn't want to see his grandma. All I wanted was for him to pull me into his arms and hold me close while I cried.

While I mourned my family and what we would no longer be.

As I approached the outside corner of his house, I heard two voices. One was Logan's, and one was a deeper, more mature voice that I knew was his dad's. I'd heard it often in the past, and even though it had been almost a year, I would never forget it.

Not when that voice was responsible for my broken heart.

"I'm not going," Logan said. His voice was low and

forceful and sent shivers down my spine. What was his dad trying to get him to do? Was it similar to what my parents were forcing on me?

I heard a deep sigh and could imagine his dad's face as he stared down at Logan. "It's not a question. There's no other option. You're coming with us. We're a family, and we stick together."

My body went cold as I leaned in. I didn't want to miss a word. Logan was leaving? Where was he going?

"It's your life. I'm staying here with Gran. I've got a life I like here. I don't want to follow you to Italy. What if this agreement fails? What are you going to do then?"

"It's not going to fail. We need to go to make sure things run smoothly." His dad's voice was pricked with annoyance. Which made me smile. Logan was fighting to stay here. That made me happier than I'd been in a long time.

"Well, sounds like you'll have a lot of work there," Logan growled.

His dad sighed again, and I peeked around the corner to see them standing a few feet away from each other. Logan was glaring at his dad, who had his arms folded and was studying the ground.

"You can't stay here, Logan," his dad finally said.

Logan straightened and began to pace. "Why not? Gran likes having me here. My life is in Sweet Mountain. You may have moved on, but I don't want to." Logan paused so that he could study his dad.

RULE #11: YOU CAN'T IGNORE YOUR FAMILY FEUD

Logan's dad lifted his hand to his neck and began to massage it. "Your grandmother is going into a retirement home as soon as you leave."

Logan stopped moving. His brow furrowed. "What?"

"She's been waiting because you're here, but it's time. She's tired of taking care of this big house all by herself." His dad glanced around. "But she won't go if she thinks you're unhappy. Are you going to do that to your grandmother?"

Logan stared at his dad for a moment before he turned away. I saw his expression fall as he scrubbed his face. "Why didn't she tell me?"

"She doesn't want to disappoint you."

The silence that followed was almost deafening as it settled around us. I stifled the sob that threatened to erupt inside of me. Why had I thought this—whatever this was between Logan and me—was going to be neat and tidy, all wrapped up in a pretty, little bow?

We were idiots to think we could make this work. We were doomed from the start.

A tear slid down my face, and suddenly, I was exhausted. This. Everything that had to do with the Cartwrights exhausted me. I was tired of fighting. I was tired of caring.

I'd had a handle on everything until Logan came blowing into my life and ruining all my hard work. I'd gotten to a place of indifference, and he shook that up.

Logan's dad gave him a curt nod and then headed up

the stairs, the sound of the back door shutting reverberated in my ears. I wanted to go to Logan—I hated how his shoulders were slumped, how he looked so broken—but I didn't.

I stood there, attempting to get a grip on my emotions, before I walked over to him and made his decision much easier.

By the time I had gathered enough courage to approach him, Logan had his back to me and was staring up at the branches above him with his hand shoved into his pockets. I held my breath as I moved to stand next to him.

He didn't take notice at first. A few seconds ticked by before I felt his gaze on my face.

"Bella?" he asked, and suddenly his arms were around me and he was pulling me close to him.

I closed my eyes for a moment as I allowed the feeling of his body pressed to mine to wash over me. I could feel my tears burning my eyes again, but I fought against them. I wasn't going to cry anymore. I was going to be strong.

When he pulled back, he stared down at me with an expression that made my heart hurt. Especially when I was about to do what my heart was begging me not to, but my head knew was right.

"When did you get here?" he asked as he furrowed his brow.

I swallowed and took a step back. "About ten minutes

ago." I kept my gaze focused on his t-shirt, unable to meet his gaze.

"You did?"

Tears brimmed my eyelids as I nodded. "I heard what your dad said." All of my emotions exploded, causing my voice to crack.

Logan dropped his hands from my arms and stepped back. He studied me as he parted his lips. I could tell he was trying to figure out what to say. And I hated it. A relationship built on this much pain was never going to last. We were doomed from the start.

I gathered my courage as I glanced up and met his gaze. Then I offered him an encouraging smile. "You need to go," I said.

Logan's frown deepened as he stared at me. "What?"

I sighed as I rubbed my temples with my fingers. Why couldn't he just make this easy? He had to know we were never going to work out. "You can't stay here. Your family wants to move on. Your grandmother wants to move on. Staying here, in a town with so much history, can't be good for you." I gave him a soft smile even though I was breaking inside.

His expression didn't change. "Are you serious?" he asked.

I sighed. "Logan, what did you think was going to happen? My family hates yours. Your parents are determined to continue down the path they took a year ago. long time ago. Did you think that our story was just going to end with happily ever after?" If I needed to be the rational voice in all of this, I would.

He began to shake his head. "I can't believe that this is how you feel. What does it matter what our families think?" He stepped closer to me and wrapped his hand around my arm. "What do you want?"

My entire body felt as if it had come to a screeching halt. It had been a long time since someone asked me what I wanted—even myself. I'd grown accustomed to the fact that I wasn't going to actually get what I wanted, so why think about it?

I wasn't sure what to say, but one thought rose to the surface. It was something I'd wanted for a long time and didn't think I could have again.

"I want to be happy again." The words rushed from my lips, and my heart pounded.

Logan stepped forward with an earnest expression. "Then let's be happy."

A tear slid down my cheek, and I angrily wiped it away. These thoughts, these words, were what got me in trouble before. They encouraged me to hope. The thought that we could have some semblance of happiness was breaking me inside.

Because I knew the truth. We weren't meant to be happy.

So I gathered my courage and stepped away from Logan. "I can't do this," I whispered.

Logan furrowed his brow. "What?"

I raised my hands, hoping he'd understand what I was failing to say. I wanted him in my life. I needed him in my life. But that was exactly why I needed to walk away. If I let him in. If I fell harder than I had already, I was going to shatter into a million pieces, and I would never recover.

I took in a deep breath and met his gaze head-on. I held it for a moment. "Please, just let me go."

Logan's gaze never left my face. Then he took a deep breath. "Is that what you want?"

I wanted to yell at him. I wanted to beg him to fight for me. I wanted to wrap my arms around him and never let him go. But I knew I couldn't do that. Our breakup was inevitable. I was just hitting it with a preemptive strike.

"Yes."

He paused, and I could feel his question in his gaze. He wanted to know why. He wanted to stop me. But I couldn't let him. If I did, I was never going to be able to let him go.

"So these last few days were what? A joke?" He stepped back and folded his arms across his chest.

I stared at him and nodded. "Well, not a joke," I whispered.

His scowled deepened. "Then what were they, Bella? They meant a lot to me, but apparently they meant nothing to you."

Tears began to well up again, and I fought hard against them. "They were..." My thoughts trailed off as I attempted to find a way to describe what had happened between us that wouldn't break his heart, but also wouldn't encourage him to think there was a chance.

He gave me an expectant look, and I swallowed my fear.

"They were..." I tried again.

"Yes?"

"They were...a mistake." The words left my lips in a whisper. I glanced up to gauge Logan's reaction.

He was staring at me with hurt written across his face. A moment later, he turned and made his way to the back stairs. "Goodbye, Bella," he said.

He took one last look at me and then grabbed the door handle. He disappeared inside. The sound of the handle engaging was the last thing I heard.

And then I was alone.

I wrapped my arms around my chest as I ducked my head and hurried over to my car. Once I got inside, I backed out of his driveway and drove down the street. I didn't let myself stop until I was parked in front of Gigi's house.

After I turned off the engine, the dam broke inside of me. I leaned forward and rested my forehead on the steering wheel and sobbed.

Sure, it had been a mistake letting Logan in. It had been a mistake allowing myself to think that things could be different between us. It had been a mistake to hope that we could have the normal guy-meets-girl relationship that we wanted. But there was a part of me—a very tiny, buried-down-deep part—that didn't regret it.

Being with Logan had made me happier than I'd been in a long time. And no matter how we ended, I wasn't going to forget that. I wasn't going to forget him.

CHAPTER FOURTEEN

Logan

I stepped into Gran's house and shut the door behind me. I collapsed against the wall and tipped my head back. My heart was aching. Anger coursed through me like lava, and it was taking all my strength not to walk up to Dad and punch him in the face.

If he hadn't come, Bella would have never heard our conversation. If Bella had never heard our conversation, then she would still be here. She would still be mine.

But now, because of my father, Bella was walking away from me once more.

My hands clenched as I heard Dad's voice. It carried from the living room. He and Gran were in a fight, and I stilled my body so I could listen.

"That boy likes her," Gran said.

I tipped my ear in the direction of their conversation. Whatever they were saying, I wanted to hear every word.

"Logan and Bella? No. Not possible. Logan would never betray us like that."

I scoffed, which relaxed my jaw muscles. Apparently, I'd been clenching the muscles so hard that, once I released them, they throbbed.

"This is ridiculous. The fight between you two families. You need to march over to the Davenports and put things right."

Leave it to Gran to give a no-nonsense answer to Dad. He needed it. He was the one at fault even though he seemed determined to make it seem otherwise.

"Regardless, he's coming with us. He can't stay here alone, and you're leaving."

My ears perked up, and I waited to hear Gran's response. Was she really leaving? Or had this been some elaborate ploy by my father to get me to agree to come? With how he behaved, I wouldn't put it past him.

"You should still ask him. Not demand it, but ask. If you don't, you might just lose your son."

I blew out my breath as I tipped my gaze toward the ceiling. This wasn't what I wanted at all. I'd come to Sweet Mountain with the hope of moving forward. Of possibly reuniting our families. But now, it seemed like that desire was far from reality.

"I'm going to bed. We're leaving in the morning."

Dad's voice grew faint as his footsteps sounded on the stairs leading to the second floor.

I waited until I heard his door close before I made my way into the living room to find Gran sitting on her chair with her forehead in her hand. Her breathing was shallow, and I worried for a moment that she was asleep.

I didn't want to wake her, but I also didn't want to leave before talking to her. She was the only rational person in my life right now. If she said to move on, to get onto the plane with Dad, I would.

I trusted her that much.

I bent forward and tried to catch a glimpse of her eyes. They were closed. She was asleep, and I wasn't going to be a jerky grandson and wake her up. I tiptoed past her. Just before I began to climb the stairs, she lifted her head.

"You're not going to talk to your grandmother?" Her voice halted my steps.

I shot her an apologetic smile. "Sorry. I thought you were sleeping."

Gran sighed as she straightened and turned her attention to the side table next to her. She lifted her mug to her lips and took a sip.

"I'm always sleeping. Gotta take advantage of those moments." She waved toward the couch. "Sit."

I nodded and made my way over to my normal spot. I leaned back, brought my ankle up to my knee, and let out my breath. Up until this point, I felt like I'd been holding it. Ever since Bella walked away, it seemed like an elephant was sitting on my chest, crushing me.

"What do you think about Italy?" Gran's voice was gravelly and rough.

I furrowed my brow. "I hate it. I don't want to go. I want to stay—"Dad's words shot through my mind, and I pinched my lips closed. If Gran wanted to go to the retirement home, I didn't want to be the reason she didn't.

Gran must have noticed my restraint because she waved my words away as she took another sip from her mug. "I'm going whether you're here or not. That wasn't fair of your father to pressure you like that." She set her mug down again.

I chuckled as I eyed her. She was always blunt, and I loved that. It helped put my mind at ease that she was determined to continue to live her life how she wanted, no matter what. It took the pressure off of me.

"I bet I can crash on Trenton's couch for the rest of the year."

When Gran didn't respond right away, I glanced over at her. Her brows lowered, and I could tell she was formulating a thought.

"What?" I asked cautiously.

My question didn't snap her out of her thoughts, and it took a moment before she responded. "What if you didn't stay? What if you went with your parents?"

I groaned. Not her too. "Why would I do that?"

Gran glanced over at me. "Your birthday is next month, right?"

I nodded.

"And you'll be eighteen?"

I nodded again.

"Then you'll be an adult and can do whatever you want. If you stay now, you'll have to get forms filled out and have your parents' permission. If you wait until you're eighteen, you can leave whenever you want."

I dropped my foot to the floor and rested my elbows on my knees as I leaned forward. I liked what she was saying. Getting out from under my parents' thumb made sense. My thoughts instantly turned to Bella, and my desire to stay grew before my head shut it down.

She'd told me to go. She'd said that we were a mistake. I was sure she was determined to not care if I left. If I was going to do this, it would be for me.

Returning to Sweet Mountain would be for me.

I glanced up to see Gran smiling at me. Her eyes were kind. Even though I was exhausted and my heart was broken so bad that I doubted it would ever be put back together, I smiled back at her.

"I'm gonna miss you," I said as I strode across the room and pulled her into a hug.

She hugged me back. When I pulled back, her eyes were glistening with tears. She hastily wiped them away. "Ridiculous allergies," she murmured.

I chuckled as I straightened. I was going to miss her.

Out of all the adults in my life, she was the most consistent. She was the one who made the most sense.

"I love you too, Gran," I said.

She hesitated for a moment before she glanced up at me. Then she blew out her breath. "I just don't want to see you become something you weren't meant to become," she whispered.

When I furrowed my brow, she continued, "What I mean to say is that I don't want to see you become a product of your parents, who can't seem to figure out which direction to go. Which direction a decent human being should go."

She waved her hand in the direction Dad had gone. "They can't see what they did to the Davenports, and I hope you never take after them." She reached out and grabbed my hand. She patted it a few times and smiled up at me. "You're better than that."

My throat tightened as I swallowed against the emotions there. Gran was right. I didn't want to live my life with regrets. Sure, Dad wasn't seeing them now, but in the future, I had a feeling all he was going to have are regrets.

"Thanks," I said, my voice softened.

Gran gave my hand a few more pats. "Well, head up to bed. You have an early flight tomorrow and lots to do." Just as I turned to walk up the stairs, she tightened her grip. "Things will be different when you come back."

Confused, I glanced over my shoulder to see Gran staring up at me. "What?"

She pressed her lips together for a moment before she offered me a soft smile. "With Bella. Things will be different. Just give her space. When you come back, approach her again."

I hated the hope that rose up inside of me at Gran's words. I was ready to put my feelings for Bella to rest. I was ready to walk away and try to just be grateful for what we had. In an act of desperation to save my breaking heart, I shook my head.

"I think that ship has sailed."

"The heart isn't so tricky, after all," she said with a sly smile.

Leave it to Gran to talk cryptic. "What?"

She shrugged. "Despite her anger, a heart wants love. That's why it finds its way to heal." She peered up at me. "Bella's heart will soften. Just don't give up."

My body flushed with warmth at Gran's words. I wanted to believe what she said was true. I wanted to hold onto the hope that, someday, Bella and I could move past the sins of our parents. That we could find the happiness we longed for in each other—I just wasn't sure if it was possible.

For now, I was going to squelch that flicker of want that was lit inside of me.

"Thanks," I said as I bent down and kissed Gran's cheek.

She chuckled and patted my hand. "Good night, Logan."

I nodded as I turned and headed up the stairs and into my room. After I shut the door, I collapsed on my bed. I was tired and ready to put this entirely confusing day to rest. Tomorrow, I would head to our New York apartment with Dad and pack up. Then we'd be on a plane to Italy.

As soon as I turned eighteen, I was out of there.

I was going to live my life for one person.

Me.

CHAPTER FIFTEEN

Bella

The last week of summer vacation flew by, which I was grateful for. After Logan left, I was pretty sure I was going to break, but thanks to Gigi, the car wash fundraiser, and work, I didn't have much time to think about him...to miss him.

I filled every minute of my days with things to keep my mind occupied.

Coach Meyer was happy to report that we'd hit the number for our trip to Brazil. She was giddy with excitement as she hurried me out of her office and off to practice.

And to tell the truth, I was excited as well. As crappy as the summer ended, I was ready to focus back on my life and my college applications. I was ready to get out of

RULE #11: YOU CAN'T IGNORE YOUR FAMILY FEUD 151

Sweet Mountain and away from my parents who couldn't seem to get their crap together.

After Dad confronted Logan, he left. A week later, he filed for a divorce. Mom spiraled for a bit, but one morning, she woke up dressed and sober. She informed me she was going out to look for a job—one that hadn't been privy to her drinking—and not to expect her home anytime soon.

I was sitting at the counter eating cereal when she told me that. I almost dropped my spoon as I stared at the put-together mom standing in front of me. I wasn't going to hold my breath that she'd really changed, but things were starting to look up.

I managed to forget Logan for the most part. It wasn't until I was lying on my bed at night, when I allowed my mind to wander, that he would unwillingly enter my thoughts. Then I would tear up at the thought of what we had. What I'd broken.

I tried so hard to hate Logan after he left, and for the first few weeks, I'd been able to hold on to that anger. But now, as I lay on my side, staring at the glowing numbers on my alarm clock, I was forgetting how to hate him. All I could feel was sadness. Sadness that I yelled at him. That I blamed him for something that was out of his control.

And if I were honest, truly honest with myself, I missed him. I wanted to know how he was doing, and if he was enjoying Italy. I found myself typing a text only to immediately delete it.

I doubted he wanted to hear from me.

Gigi got sick of my moping. She'd constantly complain that I was a killjoy and tell me to either call Logan and apologize or get over him with any other eligible bachelor in Sweet Mountain High. I would laugh and joke with her, but inside I was dying. I didn't want anyone else. I wanted Logan.

I just didn't know how to tell him that.

It wasn't until the Friday before homecoming that the school started to buzz. I was on my way to my last period when Gigi raced up to me and linked arms. She pulled me—unwillingly—into the first-floor girl's bathroom and whipped around to face me.

"Bella," she said, her voice light and breathy from exertion.

I studied her. "What?" I asked, mimicking her.

She glared at me. Then she pushed her long hair from her face. It felt like an eternity before she spoke. Almost as if she were debating whether or not she should speak. Finally, a sweet smile spread across her lips as she shrugged. "Wanna blow off last period and go shopping? I have some last-minute things to pick up for tomorrow."

I stared at her and then chuckled. "That's why you pulled me away like a mad woman?" I asked as I turned to the mirror and began inspecting my face.

"Yep, that's the reason. So, what do you say? Ditch with me?"

I peered over at her and sighed. What else did I have

RULE #11: YOU CAN'T IGNORE YOUR FAMILY FEUD   153

to lose? Last period was a study hall anyway. I gave her a smile and nodded. "Sure. Why not?"

She giggled as we linked arms and left the bathroom. After four hours at the mall, she dropped me off at my house and told me she'd meet me at the homecoming game. To be completely honest, going to a football game was the last thing I wanted to do, but it beat sitting in my empty house, alone.

The next morning, Mom was in bed. Not wanting to wake her up, I hurried to gather my stuff for homecoming and headed over to Gigi's house. She screamed when she opened the door.

Neither of us had dates, so we'd agreed to go together. Gigi had the whole day planned out. We were going to watch chick flicks and pamper ourselves. Then we were headed to a fancy restaurant, and then to homecoming, where, as Gigi put it, we were going to dance our butts off.

I'll admit, I was looking forward to it. I needed to have some fun, and hanging out with Gigi was always a good time.

By the time evening rolled around, I felt amazing. My skin had never been this soft. My nails were painted—toes and fingers. My hair was curled and pulled back. And the dress I'd picked was simple but elegant. It was a boat cut with short sleeves. It hugged me around my hips and flared out right above my knee.

I'd never worn anything this fancy before, but Gigi

had insisted that I buy it. She said it was a treat I deserved to give myself.

And I had to admit, it was nice to pamper myself. I'd spent so much of my life on soccer and school that I never took the time to just enjoy the moment. I was going to make this my new life mission, to not only survive but *live*. Have fun. After all, what was the point of living if I wasn't enjoying myself?

I leaned forward and studied my reflection in Gigi's vanity. She'd stepped out for a few minutes, saying she'd left something in her car. I ran my hand over my curls and marveled at the way Gigi got them to stay in my hair.

In the distance, I heard the doorbell ring. I furrowed my brow as I looked over my shoulder. Where was Gigi? Did she lock herself out again?

I sighed as I straightened and made my way to the stairs. Once I was on the main floor, I laughed as I walked over to the door, only to find it unlocked.

Confused, I turned the handle and pulled the door open.

The entire room turned upside down when my gaze landed on Logan. He was standing in front of me in a suit and held a small plastic container with a flower inside of it.

My brain was trying to catch up with what was happening, but I couldn't seem to process anything. What was going on? Why was he here? He was supposed to be in Italy. And why was he wearing a suit?

"Hi, Bella," he said. The familiarity of his voice

washed over me, and, despite my best efforts, tears formed on my lids.

"Lo-Logan?"

The side of his lips tipped up as he smiled at me. I hated that with just one look, all the memories of those few wonderful days came rushing back to me. The intensity in his stare. His cheekbones. His lips. The way he stood over me like he was going to protect me always.

A fall breeze picked up, and suddenly, I was basked in his cologne.

An ache rose up inside of me. Even though my life seemed to be getting better, I still missed Logan. I still wanted him next to me. By my side.

"I heard you needed a date," he said as he handed me the corsage.

"She does not. I told you we are perfectly happy going together," Gigi piped up. I glanced over to see her come out of the kitchen.

She knew he was back?

"You need this," she said as she walked past me, grabbing my hand and squeezing it before she disappeared upstairs.

I still had no idea what was going on. It felt as if everyone around me knew what was happening except me. Wanting to get to the bottom of this, I turned my attention to Logan.

"I thought you were going to Italy," I said, thankful that I finally revived my voice.

Logan chuckled as he shoved his hands into his front pockets. "I did."

I fiddled with the edge of the corsage box. "Then why are you here?"

His expression stilled as he studied me. Then he glanced over to the side. The seconds that ticked by felt like hours as he stared at me. "Did you mean it?"

His words confused me. "What?"

He sighed and scrubbed his face. "What you said to me the day before I left."

Still confused, I studied him.

"That it was a mistake?" he offered.

I blinked a few times. Right. I had said that. And in the moment, yes, I'd felt that way. But now? I wasn't so sure. It hadn't been fair for me to blame him for what our parents did. What his parents did.

Not wanting to lie—and not wanting to tell the truth—I wrapped my arms around my waist and turned away from him to lean against the doorframe.

I let out my breath slowly as I tipped my face up. I decided to be truthful. I was tired of living in the darkness. I was ready to step out into the light.

"Logan, I was upset. I was angry and hurt. Hearing you talk to your dad after coming from the lecture my parents gave me—it made me feel hopeless..." My voice trailed off. I could feel his stare and it took my breath away.

When he didn't respond, I peeked over at him to see that I had been right. He hadn't taken his gaze off me.

"It felt like a mistake back then. Now?" Tears welled up again, and this time, I let one slip as I closed my eyes.

The light brush of fingertips against my cheek caused my entire body to stiffen.

"Bella, I'm sorry," he whispered.

I kept my eyes closed because I feared that if I opened them he would disappear. That I would wake up from this dream and he would be gone.

"Why are you here?" I asked as I finally got the courage to speak.

He pulled his hand away, leaving my skin feeling cold and alone.

"As soon as I turned eighteen, I told my parents I was done living their life. I was tired of their scene, and I was going to choose a life that I wanted."

A sob escaped my lips as I felt two hands surround my arms, and I was pulled to Logan's chest. His arms engulfed me.

"I wanted to come back here. I wanted to start a life here, whatever that may be."

I buried my face into his shoulder. Even after all this time, I missed the way I felt when I was with him. My arms rose up, and I hugged him back. That must have been the sign he was looking for, because a moment later, he dropped his face into the crook of my neck and nuzzled me.

"I missed you," he whispered.

I nodded as I squeezed him. "I missed you, too."

He held me for a moment longer before he pulled back and met my gaze. He reached up, and his fingertips brushed my skin as he tucked my hair behind my ear.

"Will you give me a second chance?" he asked.

I held his gaze and slowly nodded. "Of course. Will you give me a second chance?"

He brought his hand up to cup my cheek as he stared hard at me. As if he wanted me to feel the weight of his words.

"I will always give you a second chance, Bella."

Before I could respond, he pressed his lips to mine. His kiss was hesitant at first, as if he feared what I would do. But I wasn't going to let him go this time. I'd walked away before, and I hated how that made me feel.

I was here for Logan, just like he was here for me. And whatever our families had to say about that, well, they didn't matter anymore.

Logan and I were going to build our relationship from here.

I slid my hands up his shoulders and entwined my fingers behind his neck, pulling him in to me. He didn't hesitate to respond. His arms surrounded my waist, and suddenly, I was airborne. He held me there, kissing me like it was the one thing he was meant to do.

It made me sing inside. Because I felt the same way.

RULE #11: YOU CAN'T IGNORE YOUR FAMILY FEUD   159

"Oh, man, I'm regretting my decision." Gigi's voice carried through the fog that was this dream.

Logan set me down, and we stepped away from each other and glanced in her direction. She was standing at the bottom of the stairs with her purse clutched in her hand.

"Are you two going to do this all night? If so, I'll catch a different ride."

I giggled as I made my way over to my best friend. "We'll be good, I promise."

Glancing over my shoulder, my cheeks heated as I caught Logan smiling at me. I threaded my arm through Gigi's and turned to face Logan. "Ready?" I asked.

Logan smiled as he stepped closer to us. "Lucky me, I get to escort two beautiful women tonight."

Gigi laughed and swatted at his chest. "Yeah, you do."

Logan smiled down at me, and I reached out to entwine my fingers with his.

"You didn't think I could keep a secret, did you?" Gigi asked as she led us out of her house.

"Secret?" I peeked over at Logan, who had a sheepish expression.

"Your little lover boy here came to school yesterday and created quite a stir. He found me and asked me to set this whole thing up," Gigi said as she glided over to Logan's car.

I slowed. Logan had his head down, and a moment later, he glanced over at me.

"You planned this?"

He held my gaze for a moment before he nodded. "It's been in the works for a while."

"It has?"

He smiled and turned, bringing his hands to my waist. "Gran and I planned this the day I left."

My eyes filled with tears again. But this time, they were happy ones. "You did?"

He nodded and leaned in to brush his lips across my cheek. "You may have thought it was a mistake, but falling in love with you was the one correct thing I've done in a very long time." He pulled back to study me. "And I wasn't going to let you go. Ever again."

A rush of emotions came over me as I reached up, grabbed the edges of his suit and pulled him to me, pressing my lips against his. I wanted him to feel exactly how I felt at this moment.

No longer were we enemies, destined to hate each other forever because of our families. We were something much more. And that was something I was never going to let go of again.

We were meant to be together. To battle the future, whatever it may hold, together. With him by my side, I could conquer anything.

Logan was mine, and I was his. And that was how it was going to be.

Forever.

***

RULE #11: YOU CAN'T IGNORE YOUR FAMILY FEUD

Want more Rule of Love Romances?? Head on over and grab you next read HERE.

For a full reading order of Anne-Marie's books, you can find them HERE.

Or scan below:

Printed in Great Britain
by Amazon